SHAKESPEARE'S SCRIBE

ALSO BY GARY BLACKWOOD

The Shakespeare Stealer

SHAKESPEARE'S SCRIBE

Gary Blackwood

DUTTON CHILDREN'S BOOKS
New York

For Lucia,
who gave poor Widge a home at last

~

Library of Congress Cataloging-in-Publication Data
Blackwood, Gary L.
Shakespeare's scribe / Gary Blackwood.—1st ed.
p. cm.
Sequel to: The Shakespeare stealer.
Summary: In plague-ridden 1602 England, a fifteen-year-old orphan boy,
who has become an apprentice actor, goes on the road with Shakespeare's troupe
and finds out more about his parents along the way.
ISBN 0-525-46444-1
[1. Theater—Fiction. 2. Orphans—Fiction. 3. Actors and actresses—Fiction.
4. Plague—England—Fiction. 5. Shakespeare, William, 1564–1616—Fiction.
6. Great Britain—History—Elizabeth, 1558–1603—Fiction.] I. Title.
PZ7.B5338 Sk 2000   [Fic]—dc21   00-034603
9/00   5-8

Published in the United States by Dutton Children's Books,
a division of Penguin Putnam Books for Young Readers
345 Hudson Street, New York, New York 10014
www.penguinputnam.com
Designed by Amy Berniker
Printed in USA
First Edition
1 3 5 7 9 10 8 6 4 2

AUTHOR'S NOTE

Several readers of *The Shakespeare Stealer*, the book to which this is a sequel, have mentioned that they had some trouble sorting out what was fact from what was fiction. (I hope that means I made everything in the book seem real and not that it all sounded totally made up!) This time I'll try to make things easier by giving you, the reader, a better notion before you begin of which parts are a result of research and which are a product of the imagination.

There really was a Dr. Timothy Bright, and he really did devise a system of "swift writing." In fact, that bit of information, stumbled upon purely by accident, was the seed from which *The Shakespeare Stealer* and its sequel grew. The passages of charactery in the books are as much like Dr. Bright's shorthand as I can make them.

With the exception of Widge and Jamie Redshaw, nearly all the characters who make up the Lord Chamberlain's Men are based on William Shakespeare's actual fellow players. Some, such as Alexander Cooke, we know nothing about except the name. Others, such as Richard Burbage and Robert Armin, were so well known that it's possible to get some idea from sixteenth-century sources of what they were like, at least onstage. William Shakespeare did have a younger brother, Edmund.

Salathiel Pavy was a member of the Children of the Chapel in reality, too, and was known for his ability to play old men's parts convincingly. All the plays mentioned in the book, whether written by Shakespeare or by someone else, were actual works of the period.

The bubonic plague was, of course, all too real. Spread in two ways—by fleas that fed on infected rats, then on humans, and by bacteria in the air—it had wiped out, by various estimates, one-fourth to one-half of the population of Europe in the fourteenth century, and regularly made a comeback. During the worst outbreaks, all public gatherings were banned. The epidemic described here actually reached its peak in the following year, 1603.

SHAKESPEARE'S
SCRIBE

*A*cting seems, on the face of it, a simple enough matter. It is, after all, but an elaborate form of lying—pretending to be someone you are not, committing to memory words set down by someone else and passing them off as your own.

I was an admirable liar. I had even lied myself into the most successful company of players in London, the Lord Chamberlain's Men. It stood to reason that I would be an admirable actor as well.

But I had since discovered that there is far more to performing than merely mouthing words in a lifelike fashion. A lad who aspires to be a player must be able to sing as sweetly as a nightingale, dance as gracefully as the Queen, change garments as swiftly as the wind changes, swordfight as skillfully as a soldier, die as satisfyingly as a martyr, and learn an astonishingly large number of lines in a distressingly short time. And if he is less than competent at any of these skills, then he must be adept at dodging a variety of missiles aimed at him by an audience that is as easily displeased as it is pleased.

I have also heard it said that, to be a successful player, one must be at least partly insane. I have no doubt that this is true. What person in his right mind would willingly endure so many demands for so little reward?

Certainly anyone who found himself behind the stage at the Globe Theatre just before a performance would have readily subscribed to the insanity theory. In fact, a first-time visitor might well imagine that, rather than entering a playhouse, he had stumbled by mistake into Bedlam, London's asylum for the mentally deranged.

In my early days at the Globe, all the hurly-burly that preceded a performance had been overwhelming for a country boy like me. And even after a year's apprenticeship, it could still be unnerving if the level of activity was frantic enough—as it was, for example, on the afternoon when we opened a new production of *Richard III*, one of Mr. Shakespeare's early plays.

Several of the players were pacing about like caged cats, muttering their lines ferociously and somehow managing to avoid colliding with one another or with our dancing and singing master, who was practicing an intricate dance step. Mr. Pope, my mentor, was berating the man who was trying desperately to strap the old fellow into a boiled-leather breastplate that seemed to have grown too small to contain Mr. Pope's ample belly.

Mr. Heminges, the company's manager, was hastily repairing the curtain that concealed the alcove at the rear of the stage. It had been torn nearly from its hooks by our clod-footed hired man, Jack, as he struggled to put one of the heavy wooden royal thrones in its proper place. Meanwhile he and Sam, one of our apprentices, were attempting to wrestle the other throne down the stairs; the throne appeared to be winning.

"C-careful, gentlemen!" called Mr. Heminges. "D-don't d-damage the arms!"

"Which ones?" groaned Sam. "Ours or the throne's?"

I and my fellow prentice and closest companion, Sander Cooke, were in the relatively calm reaches of the tiring-room, getting into our costumes. The chaos outside did not concern me overly. I had learned that, like Mr. Heminges's stuttering, all trace of it would vanish once we were upon the stage. Then Mr. Shakespeare strode into the room, bearing a fistful of crumpled papers, which he held out to me. "Can you copy these out in the form of sides, Widge?"

Because of my skill with a pen, it was my job to copy out the sides, or partial scripts from which each actor learned his lines. I smoothed out one of the pages and peered at Mr. Shakespeare's deformed handwriting. "Aye," I said. Under my breath I added, "An I can manage to decipher them." The others in the company were fond of poking fun at the system of swift writing I had learned from my first master, Dr. Timothy Bright, calling it "scribble-hand," but in truth it was scarcely more difficult to read than Mr. Shakespeare's scrawl.

I was about to tuck the pages inside my wallet, but Mr. Shakespeare waved an urgent hand at me. "No, no, it's to be done at once."

I blinked at him in disbelief. "What, *now*, do you mean? But—but we've no more than a quarter hour before the performance begins."

Mr. Shakespeare shrugged. "Not to worry. They're not needed until Act Four."

"Ah, well," I said sarcastically, "wi' that much time at me disposal, I could copy out all of *The Faerie Queene*."

The moment Mr. Shakespeare was gone, I unfolded the sheets and stared at them, feeling dazed. "Does 'a truly expect me to copy all these lines, and the actors to con them, before the fourth act?"

"He didn't seem to me to be jesting," Sander said. "Did he to you?"

"Nay." I sighed. "I'll ha' to use Mr. Heminges's desk."

"I'll come with you and deliver the sides as you complete them."

"Thanks." As we headed for the property room, I said, "I sometimes get the feeling that I'm of more value to the company as a scribe than as a player."

"Oh, I'd hardly say that."

"I'm not complaining, mind you. Not exactly. I mean . . ." I lowered my voice. "In truth, I'd volunteer to clean out the jakes and haul the contents to the dung heap an that's what it took to belong to the company."

Sander grinned. "So would I. But let's not make it known, shall we? We've enough to do already."

There was no denying that. Our every morning was occupied with learning the essential skills of a player, our afternoons with demonstrating them upon the stage. And when we were not practicing or performing, we were engaged in some menial task—cleaning up the yard of the theatre, whitewashing the walls, polishing stage armor and weapons.

In return for all our work, we received three shillings a week, Sunday afternoons free, and, if we performed well enough, the applause of the audience. It was not an easy life. Yet I would not have traded it for any other.

Part of the attraction, of course, was the performing. Odd as it may seem, there is a satisfaction unlike any other in creating an imaginary world and in pretending to be someone you are not. That in itself may be a sign of insanity. In the world at large, after all, a wight who goes about trying to convince others that he is a woman, or a faerie, or a famous historical personage, is ordinarily shut up somewhere safe.

But the opportunity to act before an audience was not my only reason, or perhaps even my primary one, for relishing my position with the Chamberlain's Men. I had grown up an orphan, and they were the nearest thing to a family I had ever known, partly mad though they might be.

As I set to work copying out the sides, trying to strike a balance between writing speedily and writing legibly, I became aware of a sort of murmuring or rustling coming from the yard of the theatre. At first it was very like the way the wind sounds, soughing through treetops. But as it grew in intensity, it came to resemble more the grumbling of some great beast, impatient to be fed.

It was our audience, impatient to be entertained. To soothe them, our trio of hired musicians struck up a tune, and some players came on to dance a jig for them. When the music ended, there was a moment of relative silence, followed by a ripple of laughter. Mr. Armin, one of our best actors, was on the stage now, doing his comical turn, perhaps trading gibes with the audience, perhaps impersonating one of the foolish fops who turned up at nearly every performance and sat on stools upon the very stage so they might be seen and admired by the groundlings.

These dandies seemed not to mind being mocked by Mr. Armin, whose antics included tripping over the fashionably elongated toes of his shoes or getting his ostentatious jewelry caught in his cloak; pretending to doze off, then slipping from his stool and landing on his hucklebones; or dropping his rapier and, as he bent to retrieve it, revealing a wide rip in the seat of his breeches.

The audience responded, as usual, with uproarious laughter. Mr. Armin's exit was accompanied by an explosion of applause, whistles, and cheers so enthusiastic that I looked up from my work. He came capering off the stage, wearing a broad smile that vanished the moment he was out of the audience's sight, to be replaced by an expression that, while still pleasant enough, was businesslike. "How are you progressing?" he asked.

"Nearly done," I replied—not much of an exaggeration.

"Excellent. I knew we could depend on you."

I nodded. As much as I appreciated the praise, it seemed faint compared to the boisterous acclaim Mr. Armin himself had just received. "Do you suppose," I said wistfully, "that I can ever hope for a response like that?"

Mr. Armin raised his eyebrows, as though taken aback by my question. "What? The applause? The laughter? Anyone can do that. All it takes is a few pratfalls, a few jests. You want more than that, Widge. You want their silence. You want their tears."

And how, I wondered, did I go about earning that? In my year's apprenticeship I had worked as hard as any other player or prentice, I was sure, and had been awarded ever more substantial parts—Maria in *Twelfth Night*, Rosaline in *Love's Labour's Lost*, Hero in *Much Ado About Nothing*.

But for all my seeming success, in my idle moments—of which there were few—I sometimes felt an anxious something worrying at the back of my brain. At first I could not give a name to it, but in time I recognized it for what it was—a lack of confidence in my skills, the nagging feeling that I was an impostor, a sham. Secretly I suspected that, beneath all the trappings, behind all the grand lines I spoke, I was not a real actor but only a rootless, feckless orphan acting the part of an actor, and I feared that one day someone in the audience or in the company would expose me.

It was not an unreasonable fear. Just in the year I had been with the company, they had dismissed my friend Julia and another apprentice named Nick, who could not be considered a friend. Of course, there had been compelling reasons: Nick had stolen a play script; Julia had had the misfortune to be a girl in a profession that admitted only boys and men.

Though I had not gotten off to a very good start with the Chamberlain's Men—in fact, I had joined them initially only in order to copy down *Hamlet* for a rival company— my transgressions since then had been minor: missed cues, forgotten lines, and the like. Still, I did not feel entirely secure. If the company did decide they could do without me, God only knew what would become of me. Aside from my dubious skills as a player and a scribe, I had no means of supporting myself. Even more unpleasant than the prospect of being out on the streets was the thought of losing the only family I had ever known and being an orphan again.

Perhaps it was just as well that I had little leisure to dwell on my fears. The sharers of the company, for reasons they did not feel compelled to explain to us prentices, had not bothered to replace Nick or Julia. That meant that Sander and Sam and I had to double up frequently—that is, play several parts apiece.

Our only respite came when the weather made it impossible to perform. During the winter months, the weather was not a factor, for we played indoors, usually at the Cross Keys Inn. But when spring came, the company moved to the open-air Globe Theatre.

That spring of 1602 was warmer than usual, so we began our outdoor season early in May. Unfortunately, it was also wetter than usual. Only when there was a distinct downpour did the sharers call off a performance. This did not mean that we did not work. They might simply call a rehearsal instead, in one of the practice rooms. Or they might send us out to spy on some rival company, such as the Lord Admiral's Men or the Children of the Chapel Royal, who had begun to get a reputation for their lively comedies and satires.

Though we did not regard a company of children as a serious threat, neither did we wish to underestimate them. So it was that, one sodden day in June, Sander and I were dispatched to the Blackfriars Theatre to see how much of the young upstarts' reputation was deserved. Since the essence of spying is to go unnoticed, we prentices were the logical choice for the mission, for our faces were not likely to be recognized, unadorned as they were with wigs or face paint.

Blackfriars, which lay just across the Thames from the Globe, was so called because it had once been home to a brotherhood of monks called the Black Friars. The building that housed the theatre had formerly been a guest house. The walls had been removed to create a spacious hall that was lighted, on this gloomy afternoon, by dozens of candles in sconces. While Sander pursued a vendor hawking apples, nuts, and candies, I found us a seat a few rows back from the stage. My neighbor was a burly, sunburned man dressed in the wide-legged trousers and conical wool cap of a seaman. He was chewing as noisily as any cow at some substance that gave off a smell so acrid and spicy it made me screw up my nose.

The sailor grinned, showing teeth that had been brown to begin with and were made more so by the substance he was chewing. "Angelica root," he said, and a bit of it came flying forth to land upon my sleeve. " 'Tis a sovereign protection against the plague." He tapped the side of his red, prominent nose. "But just to be certain, I've stuffed my nose holes with rue and wormwood."

I felt a chill run up my back. "Why . . . ?" I began, but my throat was thick, and I had to clear it to continue. "Why take such measures now, though? The plague is no particular threat."

"That may be true here, but . . ." The man leaned down close to me, as if not wishing all to hear. "I've just come from Yarmouth, and they're dying by the dozens there. The city fathers have taken to shooting dogs, and setting off gunpowder in the streets to clear the air. It's but a matter of time before the contagion spreads to London—if it hasn't already."

I shrank back from the man and his foul, angelica-scented breath. I had known the smell was familiar, but until that moment I had not known why. Now the answer came to me in a flash of memory. I saw myself at the age of seven, standing by my old master, Dr. Bright, as he treated a plague victim. I was heating over a candle flame some concoction of grease and herbs, which the doctor then plastered on the patient's open sores. The reek of the medicine alone was enough to nauseate; added to it was the putrid stench of the sores themselves and, underneath it all, the bitter presence of the angelica root that lay like a tumor beneath my tongue, gagging me.

Now, with the same scent strong in my nostrils, I felt

nausea rising in me again, accompanied by a sickening feeling of dread. Most folk believed that the plague was caused by corrupted air. But according to Dr. Bright's theory, the contagion spread by means of tiny plague seeds, invisible to the eye, which entered our orifices and took root inside us. When they matured, they bore more seeds that went wafting, like the seeds of a dandelion, on the wind of our breath until they found fertile ground.

I sprang from my seat and made for the rear of the room, meaning to put as much distance between myself and the sailor as I possibly could. As I swam against the incoming tide of playgoers, I collided with Sander, who carried a paper cone filled with roasted hazelnuts. "Why did you not save our spot, Widge?" he asked. "It would have given us a good view of the stage."

"Too close," I muttered. "The players' spittle rains down upon you when they say their *t*'s and *p*'s. Let's move back." Before he could protest, I struggled on to the very last row of benches and plopped down. "This is good," I said. "An there's a fire, we'll be the first ones out." Agreeable as always, Sander took a seat next to me.

The play was a fairly challenging one—Jonson's satire *The Poetaster*—and the Children of the Chapel, who ranged in age from about ten to fourteen or fifteen, were sadly inadequate to the challenge. Though they tried hard to please, mugging and gesturing in an effort to coax laughs from the audience, the whole thing was more in the nature of a pageant than a performance, all surface and no depth.

I leaned over to Sander, meaning to say that I had seen enough. Then the boy who played Horace strode out upon the stage and sang,

"Swell me a bowl with lusty wine,
Till I may see the plump Lyaeus swim
Above the brim:
I drink, as I would write,
In flowing measure, filled with flame, and spright."

I sat up in surprise. Could it be that there was a real performer among them? The newcomer was tall and thin, with a head of blond curls that would have let him play any of our young ladies' parts without benefit of a wig. Though he was likely a year or two younger than Sander or me, he had the assurance of an adult actor. His voice was not mature, and it had a rough edge to it, as though he was straining a bit to be heard. Yet he spoke his lines with such authority, such conviction, as to give the feeling not only that he understood them, but that he *meant* them.

When the boy took his bow, the applause and cheers were not quite as raucous as they had been for Mr. Armin, but they were enough to make me envious. As we left the theatre, Sander said, "Was the blond fellow truly that good, or did he only seem so put up against the others?"

" 'A was truly that good," I replied. "I'm glad 'a's wi' the Chapel Children and not the Chamberlain's Men."

Sander gave me a look of surprise. "Why?"

"Because, an 'a were wi' our company, 'a'd have all the

15

meaty parts, and you and I would ha' to be content wi' scraps."

Sander laughed. "Don't price yourself so cheaply, Widge. You're as capable an actor as he is."

"Liar," I said, but I couldn't help feeling grateful for his loyalty. I said nothing about the sailor and his talk of the plague, for I was trying hard not to think about it. Instead, I said, "Did not the fellow who played Tibullus put you in mind of our old friend Nick?"

Sander considered this. "Now that you say it, he did bear a certain resemblance, though I think that Nick, for all his faults, was a better actor. I wonder what's become of him?"

" 'A's drunk himself to death, most like, or been gutted by someone in a duel."

Sander nodded soberly. "It would scarcely surprise me. I never knew anyone so determined to make himself miserable."

"Not to mention those around him."

Sander clucked his tongue. "We shouldn't speak so uncharitably of him. Perhaps he's learned the error of his ways."

"Oh, aye," I replied, "and perhaps a dunghill can learn not to stink."

The look of disapproval Sander gave me was severely undermined by the snort of laughter that escaped him. We would not have been so quick to laugh had we known how near the mark our jabs had struck.

A few days later, as we were dressing for a performance

of *What You Will*, Sam rushed in, wide-eyed and breathless. "You'll not believe what I just learned!"

Had I been wearing hose and not a dress, my heart would have sunk into them, for I expected him to reveal that there had been an outbreak of the contagion in the city. Instead, he said, "I've just been at the Swan playhouse, talking with a prentice from the Earl of Pembroke's Men. It seems they lately took Nick on as hired man."

"What, *our* Nick?" Sander said.

"The very same. But that's not the news. He says that Nick had a falling-out with one of the other members of the company, and the man challenged him to a duel."

"Gog's blood," I muttered. "It's just as I said."

"This prentice, he served as a second in the duel, and the weapon of choice was not swords but pistols."

"I doubt that Nick has ever fired a pistol before," said Sander.

"Apparently not," said Sam, "for it was loaded wrong—they put in too much powder, perhaps—and blew up in his face."

Sander drew in a sharp, sympathetic breath. "He's all right, though?" he said hopefully.

Sam shook his head. "This fellow says not. He and his man made a hasty departure to avoid arrest, but he seemed to think Nick was a gone goose."

Sander and I glanced guiltily at one another. "It's as if we wished it upon him," Sander said softly.

"Nay, don't think that," I protested. "Though I'm sorry

for him, it was none of our doing. 'A brought it upon himself."

"Widge is right," said Sam. "You know as well as I what a hothead Nick was."

"I know. But he wasn't a bad fellow. He didn't deserve to die."

We relayed the sad news to the sharers. They made inquiries but could learn nothing more of the matter. This was no surprise. Though dueling was a common enough practice in London, it was also against the law. Pembroke's Men would naturally make every effort to protect the player who had been involved, as any company worth the name would do. We could only hope that poor Nick had been delivered into the hands of the church or the coroner's office and given a proper burial.

As the second act of a play follows without intermission upon the heels of the first, the warm, wet spring gave way without a break to a sultry summer. We at the Globe were, as usual, too busy to notice. Though our company was smaller than normal, the size of our audience was, the sharers said, at an all-time high. A portion of the profits went toward having the roof rethatched, purchasing properties and costumes, and buying new plays for our repertoire. But much of the money was paid to the temporary players.

It was hard for us prentices, always having to work with someone new. But I made no complaint; I had no wish to be but a temporary player myself. It could not have been easy for the sharers, either, constantly having to seek competent actors. If a player was not already attached to some company, there was usually a reason. Perhaps he drank too much, or was a thief, or was at that awkward age when his voice could not decide between treble and bass. The situation put a strain on Mr. Shakespeare especially. He could hardly tailor a play to suit the players when the players changed from week to week or day to day.

The only member of the company I heard complain, though, was Sam, and he was not being quarrelous so much as just speaking his mind—something that, as with the lines he spoke on the stage, he did with little or no prompting. Though he lodged with Mr. Phillips, Sam often dined at Mr. Pope's, where Sander and I lived, along with a small troupe of young orphans Mr. Pope had generously taken in. Over dinner one evening, Sam said, "I hope we never hire that Thomas fellow again. He's got two left feet, or perhaps three. Did you see him step on the hem of my gown?"

"Nay, but I heard it," I said, and imitated the ripping sound.

"Is that what it was?" said Mr. Pope innocently. "I thought it was Sam passing wind."

"Very funny," Sam said. "In fact, the gown is in stitches over it."

"Well, we will not be likely to use him again," Mr. Pope said, "unless we're desperate. He tore his lines up rather badly, too, I noticed. It's fortunate you two are so adept at thribbling."

I couldn't help feeling pleased, for thribbling—that is, improvising when another player falters—was something I'd only lately learned to do with any degree of skill. But Sam was in no mood for compliments.

"Why do we put up with such ninnies?" he asked. "Why does the company not take on more prentices or hired men?"

Mr. Pope stroked his beard thoughtfully, looking not as though he was unsure of the answer but as though he was unwilling to divulge it. "There are . . . a number of reasons," he said finally. We waited, but he did not seem inclined to tell us what those reasons were.

We were not long in finding out.

When we arrived at the Globe in the morning, we found a notice tacked to the rear door announcing that, beginning Monday next, all public performances would be banned, by order of the Queen's physicians. A familiar thrill of dread went through me. "Oh, gis," I murmured. "It's the plague."

Sander stared at the paper incredulously. "No, surely that can't be it. The rule has always been that they close the theatres when the weekly death toll reaches thirty." He turned to Mr. Pope. "It's been nowhere near that, has it?"

Mr. Pope pulled the notice from the door and carefully rolled it up. He did not seem particularly upset over finding it there. He looked, in fact, as though he'd expected it. "That has been the rule in the past," he said. "But the Queen has a new chief physician, a Dr. Gilbert, and from what Mr. Tilney, the Master of Revels, tells us, this Dr. Gilbert has advised Her Majesty to ban all public gatherings *before* the plague becomes a problem."

"Oh, what does he know?" said Sam. "I've heard he also claims that the earth is a giant magnet."

"Anyway," put in Sander, "what makes him think there'll be a problem at all? There can't be more than a dozen cases a month. That's fewer than the number of murders."

Mr. Pope spread his hands in a gesture of helplessness. "Apparently this doctor of hers is predicting a bad year for the plague, based on certain signs and portents."

Sam sniffed skeptically. "What, the alignment of the planets, I suppose? Or has a comet been spied?"

"No, he's no astrologer." Mr. Pope unrolled the paper and, holding it at arm's length, peered at the print. "Judging from this, he's more concerned with conditions closer to home, such as . . . quote, 'the unusually warm and rainy weather, the abundance of fog and vapors, the prevailing southerly winds, the great number of worms, frogs, flies, and other creatures engendered of putrefaction, rats and moles running rampant in the streets, birds falling from the skies, et cetera, et cetera.' "

"Birds falling from the skies?" Sam echoed. "When was the last time you saw birds falling from the skies?" He pointed up in the air and exclaimed in a comical old man's voice, "God's blood, Maude, look—it's raining pigeons!"

No one laughed. "What does this mean for us, then?" I said glumly.

Mr. Pope carefully rolled up the paper again. "That remains to be seen. We've been expecting this; that's why we've not taken on any new prentices or hired men. But we haven't yet decided what to do about it."

They decided that very morning. The sharers gathered in the dining room of the theatre, behind closed doors, to discuss the matter while the prentices and hired men sat about, silent and gloomy, like prisoners waiting to be sentenced.

Mercifully, we had not long to wait. After no more than half an hour Mr. Heminges called us in. "G-good news. We've decided to g-go on performing."

I stared at him, not certain I'd heard him properly. "Truly?" I said eagerly. "But—how can we do that?"

"By turning gypsy," said Mr. Shakespeare.

"Traveling, you mean?" asked Sander.

"Exactly. We've done it before, eight or nine years ago, when the plague last hit London in earnest. It was . . ." He paused and, toying thoughtfully with his earring, glanced about at the other sharers with a curious, almost amused expression. "How shall I describe it, gentlemen?"

"Unconventional?" suggested Mr. Armin.

"Uncomfortable," said Mr. Pope.

"Unprofitable," said Mr. Burbage.

Mr. Heminges gave them all a disapproving look. "It was n-not so bad."

Of course not, I thought optimistically. How bad could it be, a summer spent traveling from town to town in the company of my friends and fellow players, bringing the magic of theatre to poor country wights starved for entertainment?

"Now n-naturally," Mr. Heminges went on, "the smaller

the t-troupe, the m-more economically we can travel. So, you see, n-not everyone in the company will be able to g-go."

The hope that had risen in me at the prospect of a reprieve abruptly subsided.

"Mr. P-Pope has begged off, on the g-grounds that his orphan b-boys need him—also on the g-grounds that he's getting t-too old to go g-gadding all over the country. Mr. B-Burbage will stay in London as well, t-to see to his many b-business affairs."

I could not bring myself to ask the question that was uppermost in my mind: What would become of us prentices? But as we were on our way home, Sam asked it for me. "What about us?"

"Us?" said Mr. Pope.

"Us prentices. Are we to stay or go?"

Mr. Pope gave him a look of reproach, which I took to mean that we were foolish to imagine there would be room for us in a company that was pared down to the core. My heart felt as heavy as barley bread. "Boys, boys," said Mr. Pope. "How could the Chamberlain's Men ever hope to manage without its bevy of beauteous ladies?"

His answer so filled me with relief that I was able to ignore for the moment all the other unanswered questions: How would we ever put on a play with only nine or ten actors? What would we do for properties and costumes? Where would we perform? Where would we lodge? How would we get from town to town? I told myself that I would find it all out in due time.

One thing I did learn was how long we were likely to lead the gypsy life. In past plague years, Mr. Heminges said, the theatres had been allowed to reopen in late September or early October, for the coming of cold weather, it seemed, reduced drastically the number of deaths.

That meant we would be on the road perhaps four months at most. I suspected I would not miss London overmuch. After all, I had lived most of my life in small country towns. What I would miss, though, were the things I had at Mr. Pope's: Goody Willingson's savory meals and kind heart, Mr. Pope's endless stock of theatre tales, the antics and affection of the orphan boys who boarded with us.

I made it a point to play longer than usual with the boys that evening, while I still might. To their number Mr. Pope had lately added a sober-faced girl of seven or eight who had lost both parents to the plague the summer before. Few households would have taken in such a child, but Mr. Pope reasoned that, if she had shown no symptoms of the plague by now, she never would.

I knew from my years of assisting Dr. Bright that this was probably so. But I also knew how capricious—and how deadly—the plague could be. Though I was a little ashamed of myself for it, I carefully avoided any close contact with the girl, whose name was Tetty. Sometimes I felt her solemn, dark eyes upon me and turned to see her gazing at me from across the room. Though she seldom spoke, I fancied that those eyes were saying, "You of all people should understand; you're an orphan, too."

Sander and the rest of Mr. Pope's boys seemed to have no

such qualms as I did. Her fellow orphans included her in their games and made room for her at the table without a second thought—or, I expect, even a first.

The sad prospect of leaving Mr. Pope and the others behind was made bearable by the knowledge that at least I would have Sander along. Or so I imagined.

ong after we were abed I lay sleepless, with my head full of all that had happened lately. I assumed that Sander had long since dropped off; he seemed able to lose himself in the arms of Morpheus anytime and anywhere—the sign of a clear conscience, I supposed.

But to my surprise I heard him whisper, "Widge? Are you awake?"

"As awake as a fish," I said.

"I've thought it over," he said, "and I'm not going."

"Not going where?"

"On the tour."

I sat up as if bitten by a bedbug and stared at him. In the moonlight that came through our small window, I could see that his eyes were closed, and his face had a peaceful look, as though he were perfectly at ease with his decision. I was not. "What possible reason could you have for not going?" I demanded.

"Whist! You'll wake the boys."

"Well," I said more softly, "what's your reason?"

"I'm needed here. With the company gone, there'll be no money coming in. Someone will have to provide for the boys and Tetty, and at Mr. Pope's age, it will be difficult for him to find work."

"It will hardly be easy for you. What will you do?"

"I don't know. Something."

"But surely the company will send Mr. Pope's share of the box to him."

"Perhaps. But the sixth part of nothing is nothing."

"You think it's possible we'll make no profit at all?"

"I think it's probable. I've heard the sharers talk of what such tours are like. Mr. Phillips was with Derby's Men in 1594. They were stranded in Sheffield and had to sell their costumes to pay their way home."

"But ours is the most noted company in England," I protested, "wi' the best plays. Folk will flock to see us. Won't they?"

"I hope so. But I won't risk these boys' welfare on it. Besides, if the plague does strike, as Dr. Gilbert predicts, I'll be needed even more here."

I swung my legs off the bed and sat with my head in my hands. "A lot of good you'll be, an the plague strikes you."

"I was hoping you'd know of some preventative."

"Me? What do I ken about it?"

"You prenticed with a doctor for seven years. What methods did he use?"

"Mostly a method known as Staying Away From Anyone

Who's Ill. An 'a could not avoid treating someone, 'a tied a cloth soaked in wine over his face."

Sander laughed. "Is that like washing your face in an ale clout?" Londoners, I had learned, used this phrase to mean getting drunk.

" 'A said it killed the plague seeds. 'A also advocated chewing angelica root and drinking plague water."

"Plague water?" Sander said with apparent alarm.

"Nay, it's not like it sounds. You make it by steeping various herbs in wine."

"Wine again, eh?"

I smiled, despite myself. "Dr. Bright prescribed wine for nearly anything—a sore throat, aching joints, a paper cut—and followed his own advice religiously." I sighed heavily and held my head again. "I can't see how we'll get by wi'out you, Sander. Who'll play the tall women?"

"They'll hire someone. The children's companies have plenty of capable actors, and they'll all be out of work, too."

That was true enough—with the theatres closed, players would be easy to come by. It was friends that were in short supply. "Well," I said glumly, "I suppose there's no changing your mind."

"No. I'm sorry."

"Well, that's a comfort to ken that you're sorry," I said. A feeling of emptiness had settled into me. Though I knew well enough that it was not hunger, I lit a candle and headed for the stairs.

"Where are you going?" Sander asked.

"To the kitchen. Want to come?"

"No, thanks. I'll stay here."

I scowled. "Don't remind me."

As I was slicing bread and beef left over from supper, I heard a curious sort of scuffling noise from one corner of the room. Suspecting a rat, I raised the carving knife and the candle and crept across the kitchen. To my surprise, I discovered a figure considerably larger than a rat huddled in the corner next to the fireplace.

It wore a white nightshirt, and at first I thought it was one of the boys. But then it lifted its head and I saw the dark eyes glistening with tears. I took an involuntary step backward. "Tetty? What are you doing down here so late?"

She did not answer with words, only shook her head sharply and put her hand over her eyes, whether to hide the tears there or to shade them from the sudden light I could not tell. "Goody Willingson will be cross wi' you an you smudge your nightshirt," I said, though we both knew that our housekeeper's wrath was to be preferred to most people's good humor. "Why don't you go on up to bed, now?"

She made no move and no reply. I stuck the knife in the chopping block and crouched down on a level with her, but still at a distance. "Is there aught amiss?" I asked, though it was plain as Dunstable highway that something was wrong. "Tetty? Tell me."

When she spoke, her voice was as soft, nearly, as the rustle of the nightshirt she gathered about her bare ankles. "I'm afeared."

"Afeared? Of what?" No answer. "The dark?" I asked. She shook her head. "What, then?"

She raised her eyes to mine. I nodded to her, to encourage her to say what was on her mind, then almost wished I had not, for she said, so softly I had to strain to hear, "Of the Black Death."

I wanted to confess to Tetty that I, like her, had seen the ravages of the plague and that she was right to fear it, that I feared it, too, so much that I shunned anyone who had come in contact with it, including her. But I knew that what she wanted, what she needed, was for someone to allay her fears, not confirm them. Had I been Sander or Goody Willingson, I would have folded her in my arms and comforted her. But I was not, and could not. All I could offer was words, and they sounded as unconvincing to my ears as the prating of the Chapel Children. "There's no danger. You're safe here."

"That's what my ma used to tell me," she whispered. "But there's nowhere safe."

"Nay, that's not so. You've naught to fear as long as you don't get too close to someone who has it."

"But I have done," she said, her voice faint and hoarse, "and now—" She bit her lip, and tears welled in her eyes again. "And now I've a pain . . . here." She put a hand to her throat. "That's how it began for my da."

My chest grew tight, so that I had trouble catching my breath. I was reluctant to take a breath, anyway, for fear of what was in the air between us. Shakily, I put a hand up before my mouth and cleared my throat. "Perhaps . . ." I ventured, "perhaps it's not . . . what you think. Do you have a fever? Is your forehead warm?"

She put a palm to her brow. "A little."

I nodded thoughtfully. "Will you do something else for me?"

"What?"

"Will you raise the hem of your nightshirt a bit, so I can examine your limbs?"

She gave me a puzzled look but did as I asked. I held the candle at arm's length and peered at her legs. The skin was smooth, pale, unblemished. "Well," I said. "That's a good sign."

"What is?"

"No red spots. Me old master told me that's one of the early signals of the plague—red marks, like pox or flea bites, on the limbs. Do you notice any soreness or swelling of the kernels just below your ears or in the hollow beneath your arm?"

She pressed her fingers to those places. "No," she said hopefully.

"You've not been vomiting or sweating—a cold sweat, I mean?"

"No."

"And you've a good appetite?"

She nodded. "I'm starved," she said, and unexpectedly giggled.

I stood and breathed a sigh of relief. "Well, you've come to the right place, then." I took up the knife and returned to slicing the roast. From the corner of my eye, I saw Tetty crawl cautiously from her hidey-hole.

"You don't think it's the plague, then?"

"Well, I'm no doctor of physic, but from what you've told me, I'd say you're suffering from that dread disease known as a sore throat." I set before her two slices of bread with beef packed between them. "It's not too sore to swallow that, is it?" She shook her head. "Good. After we've eaten, I'll make you up some swish water to gargle with."

She blinked her dark eyes quizzically. "What's *that*?"

"Warm water wi' honeycomb, pepper, and cloves. Mr. Phillips has me use it to sweeten me voice for singing. It has yet to work. But it does soothe a person's pipes."

Around a prodigious mouthful of bread and beef, Tetty said, "You know a lot about medicine."

I laughed. "Nay, I only act as though I do."

"Then you're a good actor."

"I hope so. I mean to make it me trade."

She gazed at me appraisingly a moment. "Do you no longer dislike me, then, or is that just more acting?"

"Dislike you? I never disliked you. I only—" I paused. No matter how many times I resolved not to lie, it seemed I always ended up needing to. "I'm not much good at making friends yet, that's all," I said, which was true enough.

Tetty nodded soberly. "Nor am I. I'm afeared—" She lowered her eyes and her voice. "I'm afeared that if I come to like someone, they'll . . ."

"They'll die?" I said.

She nodded again. "Like my ma and da."

"Don't think that way. It was none of your doing. It was the contagion."

"Then why did it not take me as well?"

I shrugged helplessly. "I don't ken th' answer to that. I doubt that anyone does."

"Was it the contagion that took your ma and da, then?" she asked.

I hesitated. This was not a subject I liked to speak of. "Nay," I said simply, "me mother died borning me." Though I had meant to leave it at that, I found myself going on. "For a passing while, like you I . . . I held meself somehow responsible for 't."

"But you no longer do?"

"Nay," I said, though it was not entirely true. There were still times, late at night, when I was tormented by the thought that, had it not been for me, she would certainly be alive yet. Of course, I still would not have known her.

"And your da?" said Tetty.

I sighed. Why was this lass so full of questions that I was so unprepared to answer? Impatient, I said the first thing that came into my head—prompted, no doubt, by the fact that we had performed *Henry VI, Part I* that afternoon. " 'A was a soldier; 'a was killed in battle, skewered by an enemy lance."

Tetty gave a slight shudder, whether from the cold or from picturing my supposed father's supposed death, I could not tell. "I'm sorry."

"Aye, so am I," I said, and I was, for having deceived her. "You'd best go on up to bed now, before that sore throat turns into something more severe."

That Saturday we gave our farewell performance at the Globe. The yard and the galleries were crammed to overflowing with folk who well knew that it would likely be their last chance to see a play until cold weather came around again and, with it, the end of the plague season.

The days that followed were every bit as hectic as if we had gone on performing. But instead of learning lessons and playing roles, we occupied our hours by packing wooden chests full of properties and costumes and taking them down to the yard, where we loaded them into one of the two carewares, or play wagons, that the sharers had had specially constructed for the tour.

Mr. Burbage, who had learned the skills of a joiner, or carpenter, from his father, had designed the carewares so that the sides could be taken down and laid across the wagon beds to form a makeshift stage. The wagons were equipped with canvas tops to keep the rain off—not off the players, I mean, but off the properties and costumes, which, unlike us, could not be easily replaced.

In addition to the paraphernalia necessary for staging our plays, we would be carrying with us wool-filled ticks and bedding, for, as Mr. Heminges pointed out, we could not always be certain of finding an inn—or, if we did, of having the money to lodge there.

Meanwhile, the sharers were attending to more subtle and less muscular matters, such as purchasing horses and supplies, obtaining our playing license, and auditioning boys to take Sander's place in the company—as if anyone could.

Though I knew I would be wise to make the most of our last days together for some time to come, I spent much of the time stupidly sulking. Sander pretended not to notice my resentful manner and went on being his usual cheerful self.

As we were carrying a heavy trunk filled with stage armor and weapons along the second-floor gallery, I spotted Mr. Armin entering the yard, accompanied by a youth who, though I had seen him but once before, I recognized immediately by his head of blond curls. I set my end of the trunk on the gallery railing and clapped a hand to my head. "Oh, Law," I groaned, "they've hired the boy from the Chapel Children."

Sander glanced over the railing at the boy, who was being introduced around to the company, and then looked back to me. "You need not look so stricken, Widge. Surely it's better to have a capable actor like him than one of those dolts we've had to put up with lately."

"Oh, aye. Well may you say that. You'll not ha' to compete wi' him for parts. You'll be *here*, playing horsey and wiping noses."

Sander smiled patiently. "Did I not tell you that you're every bit as good an actor as he is?"

"Aye, but it's not me you ha' to convince; it's the sharers."

"No," said Sander. "I think it's you."

"Let's get this down to the careware," I muttered, "before me arms fall off and they pack them i' the chest wi' the fake plaster limbs."

As we wrestled the trunk down the gallery stairs, I kept one eye on the new boy. His manner was agreeable enough. He smiled in a charming way and greeted each member of the company with what seemed sincere pleasure. When he was introduced to Mr. Burbage, he was almost reverential and, from what I could overhear, lavish in praising the man's portrayal of Hamlet, which the boy apparently had seen no less than twelve times. He seemed equally honored to make the acquaintance of Mr. Shakespeare.

As we loaded the chest in the careware, Mr. Armin called, "Widge, Sander! Come and meet our new prentice! You, too, Sam!"

Sam, who was in the bed of the wagon arranging boxes and bundles, jumped down next to me. "Looks like a bit of a lickspittle to me," he whispered.

"A what?"

"You know—a bootlicker, a flatterer."

"Whist!" scolded Sander. "Be nice, now! 'It hurts not the tongue to give fair words.' "

"Just don't ask me to hold my tongue," Sam said. "That does hurt."

We strolled over to Mr. Armin. "Boys," he said, "I'd like you to make welcome your new colleague, Salathiel Pavy."

"Salathiel?" Sam echoed. I would have sworn he was set to snicker, but he somehow restrained himself. "Very pleased to meet you." He held out a hand to Salathiel Pavy, who took it very genially—but very briefly. In a trice his charming smile had transformed to a look of horror. He jumped as if he'd been bitten, and flung to the ground the hand that Sam had offered him—for it was one of the plaster models that represented Lavinia's severed hands in *Titus Andronicus*.

Sam doubled over with laughter and Sander and I could not help following suit. Even Mr. Armin had trouble keeping a sober face. "As you can see," he said, "our boys are always willing to give a new member of the company a hand."

I expected Salathiel Pavy, once he had recovered from the initial shock, to join in the laughter and perhaps make a jest of his own in return. Instead, he turned on his heel indignantly and stalked out of the yard. "Well," Sam said, "I trust you were not counting on him to play comic parts. Clearly he has no sense of humor."

"And you," said Mr. Armin, "clearly have no sense of

tact. You've had your fun. Now I expect you to make him welcome, boys, just as you were made welcome when you joined the company. Is that clear?"

We wiped off our foolish grins and nodded and tried to look properly chastened. As Mr. Armin walked away, he called over his shoulder, "Sam, you need to work on your remorseful look. Have the others coach you."

When he was gone, Sander said, "He's right, you know."

"What was wrong with the way I looked?" Sam demanded.

"I mean about making the new boy welcome. I doubt he's ever played in an adult company before. It's bound to be hard for him."

I thought back on how difficult it had been for me during my early weeks as a prentice, learning what was expected of me, and delivering it. If Sander and Julia had not given me help and encouragement, I would not still have been with the company. It was, I supposed, my turn to do the same. "I'll fetch him," I said, "and we'll start over."

"Sam?" prompted Sander.

Sam sighed and rolled his eyes. "Yes, all right, I'll try." He screwed his face up into a grimace. "How's that? Do I look remorseful now?"

"You look as though you've swallowed a fish bone," I said. "Just look normal."

"Ooh," said Sam, "that's even harder."

Salathiel Pavy was sitting on the edge of a wooden footbridge that crossed one of the many drainage ditches around the theatre. He was looking glumly out over the Thames toward Blackfriars, as though wishing he'd never left it. I came up behind him, clearing my throat so as not to startle him. "Salathiel? Or do they call you Sal?" He did not answer, or even acknowledge my presence. Undaunted, I went on. "It seems we started off on the wrong foot." I couldn't help adding, "Or hand, as it were."

He gave me a sidewise glance that was anything but amused. Perhaps Sam was right; perhaps he just did not appreciate a jest. Knowing he must be feeling like an outsider, I looked for a way to include him. "We'd all appreciate it an you'd give us a"—I'd almost said "a hand" —"an you'd help us wi' loading the carewares for the tour."

He turned to look at me directly at last, and his expression was less hostile than wary. "Would you?"

"Aye. Those trunks get heavy," I said, flexing my aching arms.

He gave me a thin smile that was totally unlike the one he had displayed when greeting the company; it held no charm nor warmth but was cold as a key. "You'll excuse me if I do not oblige you. I was hired to be an actor, not a stagehand."

For a moment I was struck dumb by the unexpected and unwarranted rudeness of his reply. Then I felt a flush of anger. I could scarcely keep myself from giving him a slight shove, which was all that would be required to topple him into the drainage ditch. But I reminded myself of Mr. Armin's instructions to make him feel welcome. I tried again.

"I saw you perform, some two weeks ago, in *The Poet-*

aster. You were . . ." I paused. I did not wish to overrate him. "You were noticeably better than the others."

"Is that supposed to be a compliment?"

"Aye."

He tilted his head in a way that, had he been a lesser actor, might have seemed merely quizzical. He managed somehow to make it clear that he was mocking my speech. "I beg your pardon?"

"*Yes,*" I said peevishly. "It was meant to be, yes."

"Well, I'm afraid it did not succeed. If I were only 'noticeably better' than those wretches, I'd begin looking for a new career."

I was sorely tempted to suggest some possibilities—perhaps something in the hermiting line—but again I restrained myself, not without effort. When I returned to the yard, Sander asked, "Did you find him?"

"Aye," I said. "I found him a conceited ass."

"Really?" said Sam. "That's good."

I frowned at him. "Why's that?"

"Well, don't you see? We can take turns riding him."

Though Sam's comment was made in jest, it had teeth in it. The truth was, the company could not afford mounts for all of us, so only the sharers would ride. We prentices and hired men would, as usual, have to rely on shank's mare. The company had purchased teams of horses to pull the wagons, of course, but these were plodding draft animals; even if they could have borne the extra weight of a rider, we could not have stood their jolting gait for long.

The day we had set for our departure proved a dismal one, but we could not put it off, for Mr. Heminges had booked an appearance for us in Reading two days hence. It would have been hard enough in the best of weather to leave the comfortable, familiar surroundings and the folk I knew and loved best, for an uncertain existence on the road. The rain that leaked from the smudged sky made the prospect even less appealing.

My leave-taking was as different from the way I had left Dr. Bright's home a year earlier as Berwick is different from London. Back then, not a soul had seemed to care a rush what became of me. Now the young boys vowed noisily not to let me go, and clung to my clothing like burrs until Mr. Pope pulled them off. Tetty, meanwhile, stood apart and gazed at me, unblinking, as though memorizing me.

Goody Willingson tearfully embraced me as though I had been her own son. Mr. Pope left me with a litany of advice nearly as extensive as that given by Polonius to Laertes in Mr. Shakespeare's *Hamlet*. But, whereas Polonius's ultimate admonition was "To thine own self be true," Mr. Pope stressed that, above all, I should not whistle in the tiring-room, lest I bring ill luck down upon the company.

I reminded him that we would not have a tiring-room. He dismissed this and went on to tell me of a wight he had known who whistled behind the stage during a performance.

"What befell him?" I asked.

"One of his fellow players chucked a pot of face paint at

him to shut him up. It struck him in the temple and killed him dead as a duck."

"Well," I said, "that certainly was ill luck." I donned my cloak. "I must go. We're to meet at nine o'clock outside Newgate."

"I'll walk with you a way," said Sander.

Just as we were going out the door Tetty rushed up to me, pressed something into my hand, and quickly retreated. I glanced down at the object. It was a sheet of paper folded into a tiny square. I looked around for Tetty, but she had vanished. "Move your bones!" called Sander. "I'm getting soaked!" I thrust the square of paper into my wallet and caught up with him.

"You'll write me now and again, I hope," said Sander as we traversed the muddy slope to the river. "Mr. Pope says that most carriers who travel to and from the city will also handle letters."

"Aye, but how will you ever reply?"

"They've told me some of the towns you'll be playing in. I can send letters ahead, to be held for you."

"I wish you were coming."

"No more than I do. But sometimes wishes must yield to duty." He put a hand upon my shoulder. "Cheer up. Autumn will be here before you know it, and everything will be the way it was. Perhaps better."

"I would that I could believe that."

"Have I ever lied to you?"

"Nay, not that I ken."

"Go on, then." We shook hands, then he urged me toward the waiting wherry boat. As it pulled away from shore, he called after me, "Cheer up!"

I waved and feigned a smile that did no credit to my acting skills. The boat had a small canopy that shielded me from the rain. Remembering the paper Tetty had given me, I drew it from my wallet and unfolded it carefully.

It was a crudely drawn picture of a group of human figures: two fat ones—Goody Willingson and Mr. Pope, I imagined; a tall, thin one—Sander, no doubt; and half a dozen small ones wearing wide grins. Standing apart from the others was a small figure with dark hair and eyes. Beneath the picture, printed in crooked, uncertain letters, were the words SO YOU'LL NOT FORGET US.

I reached Newgate, drenched and downhearted, just as
the bells at St. Paul's rang tierce. The carewares, each with
a pair of draft horses hitched to it, sat by the road. A sheet
of canvas was stretched between the wagons, and under
this the rest of the company were gathered, looking more
like a forlorn band of vagabonds than one of London's pre-
mier theatre troupes.

We had all been issued navy blue hats and cloaks em-
broidered with our badge, a rampant swan. This livery
marked us as the Lord Chamberlain's Men, licensed to perform anywhere in the realm. But no one wished to soil this
fine livery by wearing it in such unpleasant weather, so we
made a rather motley company, and a dismayingly small
one. As Mr. Heminges had said, Mr. Burbage chose not to
make the tour. That left us with the following cast, in order of importance, as it were:

MR. WILLIAM SHAKESPEARE, *ordinary playwright of the company*

MR. JOHN HEMINGES, *business manager*

MR. ROBERT ARMIN, *clown and fencing master*

MR. AUGUSTINE PHILLIPS, *player of villains and dancing and singing instructor*

MR. WILLIAM SLY, *hired man*

MR. JACK GRYMES, *hired man*

MASTER SALATHIEL PAVY, *prentice*

MASTER SAMUEL CROSSE, *prentice*

MASTER WIDGE (NO SURNAME), *prentice*

There was, in addition, an unfamiliar face in the group. Though he was well past the age of a prentice, he had not let his beard grow. His head of black hair was worn longer than most men's and, in deference to the weather, pulled into a horse tail. He slouched indolently against one of the carewares, with a pained look upon his face, as though he would much rather have been somewhere else, somewhere warm and dry.

"Have you met my brother Ned?" asked Mr. Shakespeare. "He'll be joining us on the tour."

"Though God knows why anyone would want to," put in Will Sly.

Ned shrugged. "It seemed to me preferable to starving or dying of the plague."

I offered my hand to him. "I'm Widge." Without changing position he languidly held out his left hand to me. I gave it an awkward shake.

Mr. Shakespeare said, "Ned has been a player in London for—how long, now?"

"Nearly a year."

"The same as I," I said. "Wi' what company?"

"The Admiral's Men." Before I could remark upon this, he went on. "Lord Pembroke's Men. Leicester's Men, for a time."

I reacted with surprise. "All in less than a year?"

He shrugged again and scowled up at the slaty sky. "None was quite to my liking."

I glanced past him at Sam, who was making a wry face as if to say, "That's *his* version of it."

"I b-believe the rain is l-letting up," Mr. Heminges said hopefully.

"If by 'letting up' you mean coming down harder," said Will Sly, "I'd agree."

"Well," said Mr. Shakespeare, "whether it's coming or going, we can delay no longer if we're to make Reading by nightfall tomorrow."

As soon as we prentices had stowed the canvas sheet in the rear of one of the already overloaded wagons, the company set off, the sharers riding horseback at the head of the procession, the teams and wagons slogging along behind them through six inches of mud, the hired men and prentices bringing up the rear, wading through the wet grass alongside the highway.

The rain went on coming down—or, as Mr. Heminges would have it, letting up—steadily all day long. By the time we reached Slough we were exhausted from dragging our waterlogged limbs along. The inn where we lodged was small, so there were but two rooms available to us. The four sharers took one; we prentices and hired men were left to crowd into the other.

We set about making ourselves as comfortable as we might—all except Sal Pavy, who merely stood in the doorway, looking about with obvious distaste at the spartan accommodations. I was not a little surprised at his attitude, for, all during the day, despite the wearisome weather, he had not uttered a word of complaint; in fact, he had put on quite a cheerful face. Apparently the face had been a false one, which he could don and doff at will.

"I was never informed that I would have to share sleeping quarters with half a dozen . . . others," he said.

"Oh, you don't have to," said Sam.

"I don't?" said Sal Pavy hopefully.

"No. Half a dozen means six, you see, and there are only five of us . . . *others*."

As usual, Sal Pavy was not amused. "I am not at all accustomed to this sort of arrangement. At Blackfriars I had a room to myself, with a feather bed." Disdainfully he prodded one of the straw mattresses furnished by the inn. "This is worse than sleeping in a stable."

"Well," said Jack grumpily, "why don't you sleep in the stable, then?"

Sal Pavy flushed. "Perhaps I will." He disappeared from the doorway.

As we stretched out upon the lumpy mattresses, I said, "A room to himself and a feather bed. Do you suppose that's so?"

"I never heard of a prentice having it that soft," said Sam. "Of course, they may have given him a separate room just to be rid of him."

"I hope he does sleep in the stable," growled Jack. "Him and his airs. Thinks he's better than the rest of us."

"And perhaps," said Sam, "being an ass, he'll feel more at home with the horses."

By the time morning came, I heartily wished I had slept in the stable. What with Jack's vigorous snoring and the bedbugs and other vermin that infested the straw mattress, I spent a restless night. The sharers evidently fared little better, for when we sat down to breakfast in the main hall of the inn, Mr. Heminges proclaimed, while scratching irritably at his bug bites, "F-from now on, we use our own m-mattresses and bedclothes."

When Sal Pavy entered the room, Sam called out to him, "Well, how were the horses?"

Sal Pavy pretended not to have heard. He looked well rested and had taken care to put on his cordial face again.

"The horses?" said Mr. Armin.

Sam nodded emphatically. "He slept in the stable, didn't you, Sal?"

"I did," Sal Pavy admitted blithely. "I don't care for crowded rooms. I believe them to be unhealthy."

Out of the corner of his mouth, Will Sly murmured to me, "Particularly when they're filled with wights who would very much like to strangle you."

I snickered. "Well, 'a does have a point, though."

"How's that?"

I nodded in Sal Pavy's direction. "You don't see him scratching, do you?"

The rain truly had let up now, but the surface of the road still resembled porridge more than earth. We made such slow progress that, by the time we reached the outskirts of Reading, its church bells were ringing compline.

Weary though we were, upon our arrival at the George & Dragon we retrieved our wool mattresses and bedclothes from the carewares and spread them on our bed frames, having deposited the inn's bedding in a pile in the hall. Though we had the luxury of a larger room this time, and no bedbugs, Sal Pavy still did not deign to bunk with us. No one seemed to mind. Though he was amiable and cooperative in the presence of the sharers, when he was in the company of hired men and prentices alone he showed his true colors, and they were not attractive ones.

In the morning, after breakfast, we cleaned the mud from ourselves as best we could, given the limited washing facilities—a ewer of lukewarm water and a bowl—and dressed in doublets and breeches taken from our costume trunk, for these were the only unmuddied garments we had. Then we donned the blue caps and capes that distinguished us as the Chamberlain's Men, and set out for the town hall.

We were forced to wait half an hour outside the mayor's chambers before he could see us, but the time passed quickly, for we were once again in good spirits with the prospect of a performance ahead of us, the first one in over a week. We occupied the time with jests and with stories of past triumphs and debacles, such as players like to tell.

Mr. Shakespeare's brother Ned held the floor longer than anyone, recalling the circumstances that had led him to leave his family home in Stratford. It seems he was caught by Sir Thomas Lucy's gamekeeper in the act of dispatching one of the lord's deer. He hinted that, in addition, he had gotten a prominent landowner's daughter with child. As a result of these trespasses, he no longer felt welcome in Stratford and had come to try his luck in London, only to be kicked out into the countryside again.

His monologue was cut short by the arrival of the mayor, a heavyset fellow dressed in gaudy scarlet clothing and adorned with gold chains of office so numerous and weighty that they would surely have brought a less brawny man to his knees. Mr. Heminges stepped forward and gave a slight bow. Just as it did when he was upon the stage, the stutter that ordinarily plagued him disappeared. "The Lord Chamberlain's Men at your service, sir."

The mayor shook hands with him and the other sharers, smiling broadly as though delighted to have a company of such renown in his city. He seemed especially honored to greet Mr. Shakespeare. "Your reputation has preceded you, sir," he boomed.

"Has it?" said Mr. Shakespeare. "Would that it had secured us better lodgings, then, and perhaps tacked a few handbills up around town." The mayor laughed, but it sounded more dutiful than amused.

"We'd like to begin setting up as soon as possible," Mr. Heminges said, "if you can direct us to where we are to perform."

The mayor's smile grew a trifle stiff, and he rubbed his beefy hands together in a way that, had a player performed the gesture on stage, would have demonstrated obvious unease. "Well, the fact is, there's been a . . . a change of plans, you might say."

"Oh?" said Mr. Heminges.

"Yes," the mayor went on uncomfortably. "You see, we've had some . . . problems. Illness, you know. In point of fact, the plague. Twelve deaths in the past week alone. In view of this, I—that is, we—that is, the town council have decided to ban all public gatherings."

"Including plays," said Mr. Heminges.

The mayor nodded emphatically, setting his wealth of chains jangling. Unexpectedly, the sound set a shiver through me, for it called to mind the clanging of a bell heard long ago in the streets of Berwick, a doleful sound that was always accompanied by the cry of "Bring out your dead! Bring out your dead!"

Our brief stay in Reading was not a total disappointment. The town councillors had authorized the sum of eighty shillings to be given the company—a reward, as it were, for *not* performing our plays. Mr. Heminges was obviously insulted and would, I believe, have turned the money down had not Mr. Shakespeare's practical sense prevailed. "John," he said, "I'm afraid we cannot afford to be overly scrupulous. This will pay for a week's lodging."

So we took the money, but, like a coin tested with the teeth for its gold content, it left a bitter taste in our mouths. We moved on to Basingstoke, where, to our dismay, we found the situation much the same. The mayor here seemed less concerned about spreading the plague, though, than about offending the church. The clergy of the city, he said, were preaching that the source of the plague deaths was not corrupted air but corrupted morals, and were singling out the bands of traveling players as a particularly evil influence.

Apparently the Earl of Sussex's Men had performed at the Guild Hall a few weeks prior; handbills advertising a matinee of *The Malcontent* were still stuck to buildings and trees. The mayor said that shortly after their departure the number of plague deaths had begun to rise.

"But that doesn't m-mean that Sussex's Men were *responsible* for the p-plague!" protested Mr. Heminges, so upset that his stutter was surfacing.

The mayor refused to listen to reason. Again we were offered money to move on; this time the bribe was only sixty shillings. "Well," sniffed Will Sly indignantly, "I should certainly have thought we had amongst us at least five pounds' worth of corruption."

Two days later, in Newbury, we encountered the same attitude, and with even less reason. There had been no plague to speak of, and the authorities were determined to keep it that way. This time Mr. Heminges refused to accept the paltry sum offered us not to play. "F-fie on them! We've a license to p-perform, and perform we will, whether they l-like it or no." I had seldom seen him so cross. Normally he was as tolerant and even-tempered as Sander. He turned to the rest of the sharers with a look that dared them to challenge him. "Are you w-with me?"

Mr. Armin held up his hands as if in surrender. Mr. Phillips nodded quickly. Mr. Shakespeare toyed thoughtfully with his earring and then smiled slightly. "You're right, John. We are not beggars; we are players. Let us not play according to someone else's script."

"They'll never let us use the town hall," Mr. Phillips said.

"Then we'll s-set up our stage in the street," Mr. Heminges declared.

While the hired men unloaded most of our equipment from the carewares and stored it in the granary of the inn, we three prentices were sent through the town with preprinted handbills announcing a performance of Mr. Shakespeare's *Love's Labour's Lost*. On each sheet we had printed in ink 2 O'CLOCK TODAY ON THE SQUARE. Some we handed out to shopkeepers and passersby; others we tacked to trees and fences and the sides of buildings.

We spent most of the morning getting our lines fixed in our heads. Though we had performed the play many times at the Globe, this was a special gypsy players' version, with all the excess parts trimmed away to make it suitable for traveling.

Even though Mr. Shakespeare had reduced the number of speaking roles from nineteen to thirteen, there were but ten of us in the company, so some of us had to double up. Sam, for example, donned a wig and dress to play Maria, then doffed them to play Moth. I played both Jaquenetta, my usual role, and Rosaline, the part usually played by Sander. Luckily for me, the two of them never appeared in the same scene.

I believe Sal Pavy's lot was the hardest. Though Ned

Shakespeare was new to the company, he had at least acted with an adult company before. Sal Pavy had not. Nor had he ever had a part in one of Mr. Shakespeare's plays. Worse, he had been given but two scant weeks to con half a dozen different roles.

In my early days with the company, when I was coaxed into playing the part of Ophelia in *Hamlet* before I was truly ready, my friend Julia had made certain that I did not disgrace myself; she had gone over and over my lines with me until they stuck in my head. Though I did not care for Sal Pavy's company, I felt it would be right for me to follow Julia's example.

I found Sal Pavy sitting alone in a corner of the courtyard with his eyes closed. He was silently mouthing his lines. "Excuse me," I said. "I thought perhaps you could use some help."

His eyes opened slowly. The look he turned on me was distracted, irritable. "Help?" he said. "With what?"

I gestured at the partial script he held in one hand. "Why wi' your part, of course."

"Oh. No, I need no help." He closed his eyes again. "And if I ever did, I would certainly ask someone more competent to give it."

I had not truly expected him to be grateful, but neither had I anticipated that he would insult me. "How would you ken," I demanded, "how competent I am or am not? You've never even seen me perform!"

"You're quite wrong," he replied calmly. "I saw you only

last month, in *Titus Andronicus*. You were . . . how can I put it kindly? . . . *dreary*."

I was not a violent person, but if I had had a sword in my hand at that moment, I would surely have thrust it through his heart—or at least considered it. When I recounted the scene for Sam, he shook his head in disgust. "The lad has a bad case of swollen head, all right. I recommend we give him a dose of the same medicine we give to Jack."

Several times in the past, when Jack had gone beyond the bounds of his duties as a hired man and insisted on pointing out our shortcomings, we had retaliated during a performance by replacing some crucial cue line with a line of our own invention. It was like throwing a lead weight to a wight who could not swim. We always rescued him eventually, but not until he had gone under a time or two.

The notion of giving Sal Pavy the same treatment was appealing; there was no doubt that he deserved it. But I reluctantly shook my head.

"Why not?" protested Sam. "It'll be great fun!"

"Because. Mr. Armin said we should make him welcome."

"Yes, well, that doesn't mean we're obliged to cheerfully accept his insults."

" 'A never insulted you. Let it pass, all right? It's not worth creating ill will over."

Sam rolled his eyes. "You sound like Sander."

"Good," I said. "I meant to."

As two o'clock approached, we set up our makeshift

stage atop the wagon beds and then returned to the inn to get into our costumes. As usual, Sal Pavy was not among us. "I expect he has a nasty case of stage stomach," said Mr. Armin, "and is somewhere vomiting his victuals."

"A little fear is good for a fellow," said Mr. Phillips. "It keeps him from getting over confident."

As we headed for the town square, Sal Pavy caught up with us. He certainly did not look as though he had spent the last hour or so puking and agonizing. He looked, in fact, as cool as a cowcumber.

"Don't tell me," Sam said. "You got dressed in the stable."

"Yes. I'm accustomed to having a modicum of privacy."

"Weren't you afraid the horses would look at you?" Sam teased. Sal Pavy ignored him. "I suppose at Blackfriars you had your own private tiring-room?"

Sal Pavy smiled smugly. "As a matter of fact, I did."

A crowd of a hundred or more townfolk had gathered before the wagon-stage, drawn by the notes of Mr. Phillips's pennywhistle. While the rest of the company went behind the striped curtain we had suspended at the rear of the stage, we prentices passed among the audience with our caps in our hands, calling "One penny, please"—or rather Sam and I did. Sal Pavy stood off to one side, silent and unmoving, with his cap held in both hands as though he found the prospect of actually soliciting money too demeaning. "Another thing he's not accustomed to, I expect," Sam muttered.

As I reached the rear of the crowd, I heard a commotion

from down the street and glanced up to see a body of eight or nine men striding purposefully toward us, wearing grim looks on their faces and carrying cudgels in their hands.

"Gog's blood!" I breathed. "They've come to run us off!" I pushed back through the crowd, raising cries of indignation, and scrambled around to the rear of the stage, where the players were waiting to make their entrances. "There's a bunch of wights wi' wasters coming!" I blurted between gasps. "I think it's the catchpolls!"

"C-constables, you mean?" said Mr. Heminges calmly. "I'll s-speak to them." He stepped through the curtain. I peered over the edge of the stage. The band of constables were dispersing the crowd, yelling, "Go home!" and brandishing their clubs.

"Gentlemen!" Mr. Heminges called in his best Pilate's voice over the clamor of the audience. "This is a lawful assembly! We are a licensed theatrical company! If you question that, we have here a decree issued by our patron, Lord Cobham!" He withdrew a paper from his wallet and began to read in a voice as mellifluous and dramatic as though he were reading the player's speech from *Hamlet*.

"To all justices, mayors, sheriffs, constables, headboroughs, and other officers, greeting. Know ye that I have licensed these my servants and their associates to freely exercise the art of playing comedies, tragedies, and histories—"

He got no further, for two of the catchpolls had climbed onto the stage and seized him by the arms. Despite his protests and those of the audience, they dragged him to the edge of the stage—not an easy task, for Mr. Heminges was not nearly as old nor as frail as he appeared in his guise of Ferdinand, King of Navarre.

One of the constables cried, "Stop struggling, old man!" and raised his cudgel. Before it could descend, Mr. Armin was through the curtains and across the boards. As quick as a dog can lick a dish, he had Mr. Heminges's rapier out of its sheath and pointing at the constable's throat-bole.

Though the sword was blunted, it would have gone badly for the man had he not let his cudgel drop. His fellow officer, taken aback by this turn of events, had loosened his grip. Mr. Heminges elbowed him sharply in the stomach and he toppled from the platform, waving his arms wildly.

Now the rest of the catchpolls were swarming onto the stage, scowling and shouting in anger. Mr. Armin booted his adversary off the apron, and he and Mr. Heminges backed away, into the ranks of the other players, who had now made an entrance en masse, with their stage swords drawn. The battle was joined.

The fight that ensued was nothing like scriming on the stage. There was no elegant, choreographed swordplay, no dramatic cries of "Have at you, now!" or "Yield, cur!"— only blows and grunts and curses. At first our men held their own, but when the officers discovered that our stage swords were more dull than deadly, the tide quickly turned.

Ned Shakespeare was the first to fall. He was struck in the ribs by a constable's cudgel and doubled up, gasping for air. His brother rushed stage left to come to his aid, but was in turn felled by a blow to his forearm that made a sickening crack, audible even over the sounds of the struggle. Mr. Shakespeare gave a bellow of pain, dropped his weapon, and sank to his knees, clutching his arm to his chest.

As I was in ladies' attire, I had no weapon save the stones

at my feet. I scooped up a handful and let one fly at Mr. Shakespeare's attacker. The man staggered downstage, holding his neck and howling. I loosed more stones whenever there was no danger of my hitting one of my fellows, and a few of them hit their mark, but it made no difference in the outcome.

Within five minutes' time, all our company were sprawled upon the stage, holding their bruised limbs and pates—all save Mr. Armin. He was backed up against the curtain with a dagger in one hand and a rapier in the other. But the look on his face, a sort of gleeful menace, was far more daunting than those dull weapons were.

The clump of catchpolls backed off, all breathing heavily, and many of them nursing wounds of their own. The largest of the men, who seemed to be their leader, took a moment to get his wind, then growled, "If it was up to me, I'd throw the lot of you in jail, but the mayor says only to make sure you leave town—as speedily as possible." He glanced up at the clock on the town hall; it read a quarter past two. "You've got until three o'clock. Then we come back." He nodded to his men. They swung to the ground—more gingerly, for the most part, than they had ascended—and departed the square.

One by one our men got to their feet, wincing and groaning. Mr. Heminges's doublet was torn; Mr. Phillips's head was bleeding; Will Sly was holding a red-stained kerchief to his mouth and muttering muffled curses; Mr. Shakespeare was cradling his right arm against his body, his face drawn and white with pain.

I glanced around for Sam. He emerged from beneath the stage. In one hand he held the cudgel that one of the constables had dropped; in the other he clutched my cap and his, which sagged under the weight of the coins we had collected. "Sorry I didn't join the fray," he told the others. "I thought I'd do better to guard the box."

Mr. Heminges smiled wanly. "G-good lad. But we m-mustn't keep the m-money, for we've not earned it."

"Not earned it?" Sam protested. "I'd say the audience got treated to quite a stirring performance."

"But more like t-two minutes' traffic upon the stage than two hours."

"Well, we can't just give it back, though, can we?" Sam gestured at the empty square. "They've all gone home."

"We'll l-leave it with the innkeeper, then."

"He's got enough of our money already—"

"That will do, Sam," said Mr. Heminges sharply.

Sam hung his head, and thrust the caps full of money at me. "You do it," he murmured. "I can't bear to."

"Have you seen Sal Pavy?" I asked him.

"Not since the excitement began. Try looking in the stable."

As we headed back to the inn, I said to Sam, "I don't think it's wise to speak back to the sharers, as you did just then."

Sam gave me a curious look. "I seem to recall you speaking back a time or two yourself. When did you become so cautious?"

I did not reply.

We were hard-pressed to take down the stage and get the carewares reloaded before the specified time. Sal Pavy turned up and, to my surprise, worked as hard as anyone. For once, all the sharers lent a hand with the labor as well, including Mr. Shakespeare, though his right arm was obviously causing him considerable pain.

The granary of the inn, where we had stored our equipment, was the center of activity. As I was dragging a property chest from the room, Mr. Shakespeare came in, his arm still clamped to his chest, his face as white as when he had played the ghost in *Hamlet*. "Where's Ned?" he demanded of the company at large. "Has anyone seen him?"

The other players glanced at one another uncertainly, and then Jack volunteered, "I seen him a quarter of an hour ago, in the kitchen, dallying with one of the maids."

Mr. Shakespeare scowled. "A plague on him! We need all the hands we have." He reached down with his uninjured arm and hefted one end of the property trunk I was struggling with. "Let me help with that." He got halfway to the careware before his legs buckled beneath him and he collapsed in a heap on the cobbles of the inn yard.

Alarmed, I called to Mr. Armin, who was hitching up the horses. "Come quickly!"

Mr. Armin knelt next to the playwright's limp body. "He's passed out. His injury must be worse than we thought." Carefully he lifted Mr. Shakespeare's right arm and gently probed the lower limb with his fingertips. Even in his unconscious state, Mr. Shakespeare cried out. "It's badly swollen," said Mr. Armin, "and I think I can feel the bone shifting. I'd say it's broken, but I can't be sure. My specialty is sword wounds. See what you think."

"Me?" I said. "Can we not find a surgeon?"

"We haven't time. You were apprenticed to a physician, Widge. Surely you must have seen him deal with broken bones."

"Seeing is one thing," I said. "Doing is another." Mr. Armin did not reply, only gazed at me expectantly. Sighing, I put my fingers very tentatively on the arm, then jerked back as Mr. Shakespeare groaned. But even that brief touch had confirmed the fracture. "Aye, it's a bad break. It'll need a splint."

"Do it quickly, then. I'd just as soon not have to face the mayor's men again, even with a sharp sword."

"But I don't—" I started to say, to no avail. He had already gone back to his task. "I don't ken what I'm doing," I muttered, and then, because there was no one else to do it, I went about setting the arm as best I might, using soft cloth for padding and two stage daggers from the property trunk for splints, binding them in place with a scarlet sash from the costume chest. Then, with Jack's reluctant help, I hoisted Mr. Shakespeare, still unconscious, and laid him out atop the supplies in one of the carewares.

The company rolled out of the inn yard just as the church bells rang nones. Mr. Armin guided his fine black mare up alongside me. "Climb on," he said. "You've earned a ride."

Gratefully, I grabbed hold of his saddle and swung up behind him. "That splint will do for now," I said. "Perhaps there'll be a surgeon in the next place we stop, who can do the job right."

"Perhaps. But you know, no matter how well it's fixed, Will's going to be unhappy with it."

"Why? 'A'll still be able to act, will 'a not?"

"No doubt. But I expect he'll have some difficulty writing."

"Oh. I hadn't thought of that. 'A's working on a new play, then?"

Mr. Armin nodded. "He's trying. I don't think it's going very well."

I wasn't surprised, considering how hectic the past several weeks had been for us. "But . . . when could 'a possibly find time the time to write?"

Mr. Armin laughed a little, as though he found my question naive. "When the rest of us are abed."

We did not attempt to account for many miles that day, for we were all of us spent, and most were sore and aching from the afternoon's skirmish. We put up at a small inn on the outskirts of Hungerford. Mr. Armin rode into the town to search for a surgeon, but without success. The best we could do for poor Mr. Shakespeare was to fortify him against the pain with brandy and put him to bed.

Over supper the rest of the sharers discussed what our next move should be. Back at the Globe, the prentices and hired men ordinarily would not have been privy to such matters, but here on the road the distance between owners and mere players seemed to have narrowed. There was an unexpressed sense of shared destiny, a feeling that we were all cooking at the same fire—or perhaps over it.

"Obviously," said Mr. Heminges, "we c-cannot go on this way. If we are n-not to be allowed t-to perform, we m-might as well have stayed in London."

Mr. Phillips tapped the side of his ale mug thoughtfully with his fingers. "I believe the problem may be that we're still too near to London. The towns here are the very ones that, during the last outbreak of the plague, were deluged with folk fleeing the city. They have not forgotten, and they're wary of travelers. I think we'll find that, farther north, or west or east, for that matter, we'll be more welcome."

"I agree," said Mr. Armin. "Northern towns especially, such as Sheffield and York, do not have dozens of theatre troupes passing through, as the towns here do. They'll be starved for a show. Isn't that so, Widge?"

So seldom did anyone ask my opinion of anything, it took me a moment to come up with a reply. "Aye," I said, feeling myself go red from all the sharers' eyes upon me. It was like being thrust upon a stage but without being told what to say. "Those few times when a company came to Berwick or even York, it was like a holiday. Shops closed, prentices were given the day off." I scratched my head and shrugged wryly. "At least *most* prentices were."

The company laughed—except, of course, for Sal Pavy.

The matter was put to a vote. To my surprise, the opinion of us prentices counted as one vote, as did that of the three hired men. With the exception of Ned Shakespeare, who felt we would find the pickings even leaner the farther we got from London, and Jack, who was generally opposed to everything, we all voted to proceed directly to the northern shires.

"I feel certain that M-Mr. Shakespeare will v-vote the same way," said Mr. Heminges.

"He may vote as he will," said Mr. Armin, "for the will of the company outweighs the will of Will, will he or nil he."

"And the weal of the company," added Mr. Phillips, "outweighs the weal of Will as well."

Mr. Armin rose from the table and picked up one of the candles. "Well, we'll see if all's well with Will. Widge?"

As we went upstairs to the room he and Mr. Shakespeare shared, I said, "I've been trying to think of a way to keep Mr. Shakespeare's bones in place while they heal, wi'out using such a bulky bandage. 'A needs something 'a can wear beneath his costume."

"And have you come up with something?"

"I believe I have." I hesitated, unsure whether my idea would sound clever or crack-brained. "You . . . you ken how we make fake limbs wi' gauze and plaster of Paris?"

Mr. Armin nodded.

"Well, why could we not do the same wi' a real limb?"

Mr. Armin stopped on the stairs, looking thoughtful. "I don't think that's a good idea."

My heart sank into my hose. "You don't?"

His face broke into a smile. "I think it's a brilliant one. Go get what you need from the wagons."

When I removed the splint, I found Mr. Shakespeare's arm still badly swollen. I wrapped a layer of plain gauze around it as tightly as I might, though it made him squirm with pain even as he slept his drugged sleep. Over that we wound layer upon layer of gauze laden with wet plaster, to a thickness of half an inch or so. "Do you suppose that will suffice?" I asked.

"Surely. You don't want to make it so heavy he can't lift it."

We bound the plastered arm to Mr. Shakespeare's chest so he could not move it until it dried. Then I sat back and heaved a long sigh of weariness and relief. "I hope it works."

"It will." Mr. Armin accompanied me into the hall. "I expect you're looking forward to making a triumphant return to Yorkshire."

"Triumphant?" I said.

"Well, you're a member of—if I may say so—the most renowned theatre company in the kingdom. Surely that will impress all your old friends and your kin."

I shrugged. "I've no kin there that I'm aware of—and no friends, either, save Mistress MacGregor at the orphanage, who gave me a name."

"She had no notion who your parents might be?"

"Not a hint. She once said me mother died in the poorhouse, giving birth to me, and that's th' extent of it."

"It must be a sad thing, always having to wonder."

"Not sad so much as frustrating. I mean . . ." I hesitated. I had never spoken of this to anyone before, not even Sander. But I was weary, and my guard was down. "I mean, wi'out any sense of who they were I've only half a sense of who *I* am. It's not just that I don't ken me proper name. It's that I don't ken what . . . what I'm made of, you might say."

Mr. Armin nodded. "Well, I've always thought that what you're made of is not as important as what you do with it."

"Aye," I said halfheartedly. "I suppose that's so." I knew he meant well, but I did not think he truly understood.

As I turned to go, he patted my shoulder in a way that put me in mind of Sander. With a sharpness and a suddenness that startled me, I found myself wishing that Sander were here. The days since we left London had been so exhausting and eventful, I had scarcely given a thought to him or to the rest of Mr. Pope's household.

Recalling Tetty's picture, I fished it from my wallet, unfolded it carefully, and gazed at it for a long while. Then, even though I was even more exhausted than usual, thanks to the nerve-racking business of binding the broken arm, I shuffled past the room where the prentices and hired men were sleeping and on down the stairs. I borrowed pen and paper from the innkeeper's wife and managed to put down nearly a page to my friend about the company's fortunes before Morpheus made my nodding head droop onto the paper. Not wishing Sander to fret, I did not write how sorely I missed him.

9

By the time we set out from Hungerford the next morning, Mr. Shakespeare was strong enough to ride, though he had to have a bit of help in mounting. The effects of the alcohol he had consumed the night before seemed to bother him as much as the arm did. Though he pronounced my plaster bandage satisfactory, I was not satisfied, for I could see how hard his swollen flesh pressed against it, and I knew it must be painful. He dismissed my concern. "The swelling will go down in a day or two," he said.

But that evening, when Mr. Shakespeare summoned me to his room at the King's Head in Wantage, I found the arm as swollen as ever. Mr. Shakespeare was clearly suffering; he had a glass of brandy at hand to ease the pain. "Perhaps I did something wrong," I said anxiously. "Perhaps I should cut the bandage off again."

"No," Mr. Shakespeare insisted. "But there is something you might do for me."

"Name it," I said, assuming he meant for me to fetch him more brandy or the like.

"Have you ever taken dictation?"

"Dictation? You mean, writing down the spoken word?"

"Exactly."

"Well . . . aye. Dr. Bright often asked me . . ." I paused. Now that I had a clearer sense of right and wrong, it embarrassed me to admit my past transgressions. " 'A was a clergyman as well as a doctor, you ken, and 'a had me visit neighboring churches and copy down the sermons of other rectors."

Mr. Shakespeare seemed more amused than disapproving. "Steal them, in other words?"

"Aye."

"And then Simon Bass had you steal my play." He shook his head. "You've had ill luck in masters."

"Until now," I said.

"Well put. What I'm asking is not dishonest, but it may be difficult. I have promised the Queen I would write a new comedy for her, to be performed upon our return to London. Her Majesty finds that such fare as *Hamlet* and *Caesar* puts her in a melancholy humor. She prefers something more . . . lightweight." The pained expression Mr. Shakespeare now wore was, I fancied, due to more than just the swollen arm.

"So," he went on, "it is my duty as a loyal subject to

concoct something her appetite finds more digestible—a trifle, as it were, and not the more substantial fare I am inclined to prepare." He gestured impatiently at his plaster-bound right arm with his left one. "And, since I cannot possibly put pen to paper for myself, I must have someone do it for me, or else fail in my duty to my Queen. If you think you're up to the task, I am prepared to give you an extra shilling a week . . . presuming I have it to give—which, in view of our singular lack of success so far, may be in doubt. So, what do you say? Will you do it?"

The offer came so unexpectedly that I found my tongue temporarily tied. "I . . . I . . ."

"Good," said Mr. Shakespeare, apparently mistaking an "I" for an "aye." He picked up a leather-bound portfolio and opened it upon the small folding desk he had brought along. The portfolio was cleverly and compactly designed, with a pocket for writing paper, one for blotting paper, a pouch that held goose quill pens and a pen knife, even a strap that secured a bottle of ink. "You sit at the desk," he said. "I'll take the bed."

Feeling awkward and uncertain, I seated myself upon the trunk that contained the company's play books and handbills and pulled up my sleeves. "Um . . . an I'm to write swiftly, a plumbago pencil would be preferable to a quill pen."

"I don't have one."

"No matter. I do." I retrieved it from my wallet and tore

off some of the paper wrapping to expose a half inch or so of the graphite core. I glanced at the pages he had written out already. From copying out the actors' sides, I was used to reading Mr. Shakespeare's undisciplined scrawl; nevertheless, I found it hard to decipher these words. A good half of them had been crossed out. In addition, there were black blotches everywhere, as though an ink plague had struck the paper.

"They tell me," said Mr. Shakespeare, "there's a rumor about London to the effect that I never blot out a line. Obviously it isn't so." He sighed and added ruefully, "Would that it were."

One thing I could make out with ease was the title, for it was printed neatly in uppercase letters: LOVE'S LABOUR'S WON. I assumed it was to be a sequel to *Love's Labour's Lost* until I saw that, although it was set in France like that other play, the names of the characters were totally unfamiliar.

"Read to me what I wrote last, if you will."

"I'll try. 'I have seen a medicine that's able to breathe life into a scone—' "

"That's *stone.*"

"Ah. Sorry. 'Quicken a rock and make you dance . . . canary? . . . with sprightly fire and motion; whose simple torch—*touch*—is powerful to raise King Pepin, nay, to give great Charlemagne a pen in 's hand, and write to her a loveline.' " I looked up from the page. "It's a play about medicine?"

"No, no," said Mr. Shakespeare. "Only in part. The hero-
ine's father was a physician, and she uses one of his nostrums to cure the king."

"Of what?"

"A fistula."

"Oh," I said. "But . . . I don't think a fistula may be cured
wi' medicines. It needs to be cut away."

Mr. Shakespeare gave me a look that implied he'd just as
soon I kept my opinions to myself. "This is a play, Widge,
not a medical treatise."

"Sorry."

"Stop saying that. Let's proceed. 'And write to her a love-
line.' 'And write to her a love-line.' " He squeezed his eyelids shut and pressed his fingers to his forehead as if trying
to force the words from his brain. "All right. *King:* 'What
her is this?' Ahh, too many syllables, I'll wager." He ticked
the syllables off on his fingers. " 'And *write* to *her* a love-
line. What *her* is *this*?' The meter limps a bit, but it'll have
to do. You have that?"

"Aye."

"All right. *Lafeu:* 'Why, Doctor She. My lord, there's one
arrived, if you will see her, by my faith I trow—' No, no.
'By my faith and honor' is better, though it doesn't scan.
'By my faith and honor, if seriously I may convey my
thoughts, hath in her wisdom and her constancy amazed
me.' Do you have that?"

"Aye, every word."

"Let me see."

I held up the paper and he peered at what I had written, which was

"Ah," he said. "You've used your . . . what is it called?"

"Charactery."

He handed the paper back to me with a quizzical smile on his face, altered by a wince of pain. "How will I ever know whether or not you've gotten it right?"

"Well, sir, I suppose you'll just have to trust me." The moment I said these words, I regretted them. After all, what cause did he have to put his trust in someone who had a history of stealing sermons and play scripts?

I feared he would say as much, but all he said was, "Yes, I suppose so. Anyway, you'll copy it all out in normal script later, I trust?"

"Aye."

He lay back on the bed with a slight groan, and continued. "Still *Lafeu:* 'Will you see her, sire, and know her business?' *King:* 'Bring her on, Lafeu.' Oh, God. That sounds as though she's a platter of meat. 'Bring her *hence,* Lafeu, that we may . . . that we may . . .' That we may *what*? That we may admire? That we may wonder? Damn!" He struck the bed a blow of frustration with his good arm, which jostled his injured limb; he at once cried out and pressed it to his chest. "That was stupid," he muttered brokenly.

"Can I get you something?"

"No, no . . . unless it's a new brain, one that works."

"It sounded well enough to me," I ventured.

"Yes, well, what do you know?" he snapped. Then he sighed, took a dose of brandy, and went on more kindly, "Go on to bed, Widge. I'm not accustomed to writing scripts in this second hand fashion, that's all. It'll go better next time."

"Aye, sir." I rose and closed up the portfolio. "Shall I blow out the candle, then?"

"What? No, leave it. I'll be awake for some time yet."

As I slipped from the room, I said softly, "Good night, sir." He made no reply. From the way he was staring at the candle flame, I judged that his thoughts were elsewhere—in France, perhaps . . . or in despair.

The room where the hired men and prentices slept was stifling. I longed to open the window and let in a bit of breeze, but I knew that I would be chastised if I did, for the others were, to a man, convinced that the night air was filled with ill humors. Jack was snoring with a sound like a dying pig, and I gave him a shove with my foot. He snorted, turned over on his side, and started in snoring once more, though at a more bearable level.

With a sigh, I sank down upon my wool mattress. Just as I was drifting off, I heard Sam whisper, close to my ear, "I've got it figured out!"

"What?" I murmured.

"I said, I've figured it out!"

"Figured *what* out?" I asked crossly.

"Why Sourpuss Pavy sleeps in the stable and uses it for a tiring-room."

"Oh. Well, are you going to tell me, so I can go to sleep?"

"I think it's because . . ." He put his mouth even nearer to my ear. "*He's* a *she!*"

I gave out with something that was half a gasp, half a burst of laughter, and muffled it with my hands. "You're daft!"

"No, no, think about it! We never suspected Julia was a girl, did we? But looking back on it, it was easy to recall things she did, things she said that if we'd added them up would have given her away. Well, this time I'm adding them up in advance. One: He doesn't sleep in the same room with us. Two: He doesn't change in the same room with us. Three: He's weak as water; he couldn't even lift one end of the arms trunk. Where am I? Four? Four: When he relieves himself, he always goes far back into the woods, out of everyone's sight. Five: He didn't take part in the scuffle yesterday afternoon, you notice."

"Nor did you," I pointed out. "As for how 'a relieves himself, I go out of sight meself. I like a bit of privacy."

"All right," Sam said defensively, "explain the stable business, then."

"I don't ken. Perhaps 'a's one of those wights who talks wi' horses. Ask him, why don't you, and let me sleep."

There was silence for a time, then Sam muttered, "I don't care what you say; I think Sal is a Sally." A moment later, he added, "Ow! You've no call to hit me!"

Sam was like a small dog who, once he has his teeth into something, will not let go no matter what. At least twice a day over the next week or so, he came up with some bit of "evidence" that supposedly added weight to his Sally Pavy theory. Most were pure foolishness, ranging from the fact that Sal Pavy scrubbed his teeth with salt rather than just a rag dipped in wine like everyone else, to the way he often sat with his legs crossed.

Though I scoffed at Sam's fancies to his face, I could not help regarding Sal Pavy in a new light, weighing his words and actions as an actor does those of his character, looking for the meaning that lies behind them. There was no denying that his manner was rather effeminate at times, but that was hardly surprising, considering he was given daily lessons in how to accurately impersonate a girl. I myself had grown so used to wearing a dress that occasionally I found myself reaching down to lift a hem that wasn't there. Besides, passing oneself off as another gender upon the stage was quite a different matter from keeping the pretense up all day, every day.

On the other hand, Sal Pavy had proven himself a master of deception. Whenever one of the sharers was about, he was the very picture of a willing, eager worker. But when we prentices were alone with any sort of task, from washing the muddy carewares to grooming the horses to airing out the mattresses, he always contrived to avoid actually contributing anything.

"At Blackfriars," he said, "we were taught how to act, not how to clean things."

"Yes," said Sam, with a meaningful glance at the sword Sal Pavy was supposed to be polishing. "I can see that. You know, Widge, when we return I believe we'd be wise to apply for a position at Blackfriars. It sounds as though it bears a striking resemblance to the land of Cockaigne." Cockaigne was, I had learned, a familiar fancy among Londoners—a mythical land of idleness and luxury.

I made no reply. Though I knew well enough that he was jesting, I found nothing amusing or appealing in the notion of leaving the Chamberlain's Men.

To Sal Pavy's credit, when it came to studying for his roles, he applied himself more assiduously than any of us. I thought myself an early riser, yet often I emerged from our room at some inn soon after sunrise to find Sal Pavy pacing about the courtyard, reciting his lines under his breath and practicing over and over the appropriate gestures to go with them.

He also worked harder than most at keeping himself and his attire clean and tidy. He bathed whenever the opportunity presented itself—in private, of course—paying from his own purse the two or three pence innkeepers customarily charged for such services. Naturally, Sam pointed to these habits as further indicators of a female nature.

We were working our way northward, now, traveling as quickly as we might and stopping at the smallest and shabbiest inns to conserve our dwindling funds. Lodging of any sort grew increasingly scarce and one night, finding ourselves between towns when darkness fell, we stopped alongside the road and spread our mattresses out upon canvas sheets beneath the carewares.

Though I welcomed the chance to sleep in the open air,

some of the other players griped about it, most notably Ned Shakespeare. I had noticed that he was not chary with his complaints at any time. The meals we ate were never to his taste; he grumbled over the fact that, though he was the famous playwright's brother, he must make the journey on foot; when the sun shone, he railed against the heat; when it rained, as it did almost daily, he cursed the damp.

It was a pity we were not farmers. Had we been, we could have put to use all the earth we turned up with the wheels of our carewares. And had we been growing crops, we might have welcomed the rain that made the roads into a morass of mud. Our definition of a good day became a day when the carewares bogged down no more than half a dozen times.

Sometimes the sharers could drag the wagons free by tying extra ropes to them and adding the pulling power of their mounts to that of the draft horses. Other times we prentices and hired men had to play the part of so many Atlases, taking onto our shoulders not the weight of the whole world but that of the wagons, which sometimes seemed nearly as great.

After one such dismal day we stopped at an inn outside Grantham, and several of the company paid for the privilege of a bath. Sam and I contented ourselves with scrubbing our clothing and shoes in the horse trough. When Sal Pavy crossed the courtyard from the stable to take his turn in the bathhouse, Sam sidled up next to me and announced gleefully, "I've a plan that will reveal the truth once and for all."

"The truth?" I echoed. "About what?"

"About whether it's Sal or Sally, you dunce."

"Sam," I said with a sigh, "must you always be harping on that same string?"

"Ah, Widge, you know you're consumed with curiosity about it."

"Nay, I'm not—truly."

He nudged me with his elbow. "Come, come, tell the truth and shame the devil. You admit, surely, that there's something suspicious about the boy—if he is, indeed, a boy."

"Well, aye, perhaps a bit, but—"

"Right. So let us find out what it is." So saying, he seized my shirtsleeve with one sopping hand and pulled me across the inn yard.

"Where are you taking me?" I demanded.

"Whist! Just over here." He led me to an alcove next to the bathhouse, where firewood was stacked. In the growing dusk, I could see a narrow shaft of light issuing from between the boards of the bathhouse and laying a yellow ribbon across the rough bark of the logs. "I discovered this earlier, when Mr. Phillips sent me to fetch firewood," Sam whispered. He knelt atop the woodpile and pressed his face to the crack in the wall.

"Stop it, you sot!" I said, and tugged at the back of his shirt, though not all that insistently, I admit. Some part of me, a part I did not much care to acknowledge, wanted to know if there was anything to Sam's theory.

Sam whispered from the side of his mouth, without taking his eye from the crack, "I can see him! He's starting to strip down! There goes the doublet . . . the breeches . . . the shirt . . . the hose . . ." There was a pause, then Sam exclaimed softly, "Gog's nowns!" and, without warning, jerked back away from the crack, nearly breaking my jaw with his pate, for I had leaned up close behind so as to hear him.

I could not see his face well in the fading light, but enough to read astonishment upon it. "What is it?" I demanded, still holding my jaw.

Sam slowly shook his head. "See for yourself," he said, and yielded his place to me.

Hesitantly, feeling uncomfortably like the fellow who peeped at Lady Godiva and was struck blind for it, I put my eye to the crack. The room was lighted by a candle I could not see; probably it was on the wall against which I leaned. In the center of the room was a wooden tub, like a half barrel, and Sal Pavy, naked as a nail, was just stepping into it.

His profile was to me, and I could see well enough that his appendages were appropriate to a boy. I was about to turn to Sam and say, "Did I not tell you so?" but then Sal Pavy shifted position, so that his back was to me, and I saw what had startled Sam so. A series of long, livid scars or welts descended his back like a ladder, continued across his buttocks, and down the backs of his thighs—the sort of marks left by a caning.

I knew the pattern well, for my own frame had been similarly decorated often enough by Dr. Bright's walking stick, when I had spilled some valuable medicine or was caught filching from the pantry. But my welts had always faded after a few days. I doubted that Sal had come by his so recently. For one thing, I could not imagine anyone in our company giving such a caning to a prentice. For another, these tracks did not look fresh. They looked, rather, like a permanent record of punishments long past.

I could only speculate about how severe the beatings must have been to have blistered the skin in such a manner, and how painful. Feeling suddenly queasy, I stepped back from the peephole and nearly lost my balance.

"Did you see it?" Sam asked in a soft, subdued voice.

"Aye," I replied. "And I would I had not."

"Who do you suppose might have given him such a smoking?"

I shook my head, unable to imagine. "You'll ha' to ask him that," I said, knowing that even Sam, with his rash tongue, would find that difficult to do.

I was still feeling shaken when I went up to Mr. Shakespeare's room. I found him at the folding desk, fighting valiantly to control his quill with his left hand, and losing. His hand, his sleeve, and his paper were all spotted and smeared with ink, and the words he had managed to set down were even more illegible than his normal script, a thing I would not have believed possible.

He laid the pen down and glanced up at me with an expression that put me in mind of the way Mr. Pope's boys looked when they were caught at some mischief. "Now I understand why the left hand is called sinister. It has a twisted will of its own and cannot be made to obey." He rose and gestured for me to take his place, then set about awkwardly trying to clean the ink from his hands using a rag soaked with brandy.

"When I was a schoolboy in Stratford," he said absently,

"I had a classmate—Laurence, his name was—who was left-handed. The schoolmaster believed this was contrary to nature and insisted that, for the purposes of penmanship at least, the boy must use his right hand. Laurence worked diligently at it, but was totally inept. The master, convinced that the boy was just being stubborn, tried to beat him into compliance."

I winced, thinking of the stripes on Sal Pavy's back. "Did 'a succeed?"

"He succeeded only in making an enemy of Laurence. When we grew bigger, one day Laurence wrested the rod from the master's hand and gave him a drubbing in return, using his right hand—just to show that he could, I suppose." Mr. Shakespeare sank onto the edge of the bed and cradled his bandaged arm. "Well. You see what I'm doing, don't you?"

"Easing your bad arm?"

He smiled wryly. "Yes, but I'm also delaying, trying to avoid setting to work."

"We need not, an you're in pain."

"The arm is not to blame. The swelling has gone down considerably, as you see." He held out the arm for my inspection. The flesh around the plaster bandage was no longer red and puffy, but nearly normal in appearance.

I smiled with relief. "I was afeared I'd done it wrong, and it wouldn't heal."

"No, you did as well as any surgeon, and I'm grateful."

"What does pain you, then?"

He frowned and lay back on the bed. "This play," he said.

I did not know how to respond. I had supposed that composing plays was an effortless task for a man of Mr. Shakespeare's gifts. But he was behaving as though it were something to be dreaded, as though it required a degree of fortitude or courage he was not sure he possessed. "Shall I . . . shall I read what I transcribed last night?"

"Yes, yes, read it all. God knows there's little enough of it."

It was true. I'd put down but half a dozen speeches the previous night, before Mr. Shakespeare grew frustrated and sent me away. The play's progress, in fact, closely resembled that of the tour as a whole—agonizingly slow, with much bogging down.

We were in the midst of what was meant to be a comic scene between the Countess and the Clown. Though Mr. Shakespeare's mood was anything but comical, he went on struggling with the scene, as his classmate must have struggled to write a satisfactory Italian-style script using the wrong hand. But Mr. Shakespeare had no master standing over him with a hickory rod. The only one driving him was himself.

He pressed his hand to his forehead in that fashion I had seen so often. "The Clown says . . . The Clown says . . . Ah! The Clown says, 'I have an answer that will fit all questions.' "

As I wrote down the line, I laughed. "An answer to fit all questions? It must be an answer of monstrous size."

"That's good!" said Mr. Shakespeare. "Write that down as well, for the Countess's line."

"Truly?" I said.

"Why not? I'm not above stealing a line when it suits."

I wrote down what I had said, happy to have been of some help, however small. "What is this answer to fit all questions, then?"

"Oh, Lord," groaned Mr. Shakespeare. "I've no idea." Then he paused and, to my surprise, smiled. "Wait. Perhaps that's it."

"What's it?"

" 'Oh, Lord.' That can be made to answer anything, depending on how you say it, can it not? Let's try it. Pose me a question."

"Pardon?"

"Pose me a question—any question."

Flustered, I asked the first thing that entered my mind. "How fares your arm, sir?"

"Oh, Lord, sir," he replied in a tone that implied it was in dreadful shape. "That works. Ask me another."

"Umm . . . ah . . . how goes the play you're composing?"

He rolled his eyes and replied in a tone of great dismay, "Oh, Lord, sir!" We both laughed at how apt the answer truly was. "Come, another," said Mr. Shakespeare. Suddenly the melancholy mood that had hung over us seemed to have lifted.

I thought of an old jest that could not well be answered with a yes or no. "Tell me, sir, do you still beat your wife?"

"Oh, Lord, sir!" This time the reply was laced with indignation. "Ha! You see, it works! Write it down! Rob will know how to make the most of it." He meant, of course,

Mr. Armin, who customarily played the broad comic parts.

Now that Mr. Shakespeare was in better spirits, he went on to dictate another scene and another, at such breakneck speed that I was hard-pressed to get it all down. It was an astounding feat, really. One might have thought the words were already fully formed in his head, and he was merely reading them off.

Though he was galloping along like a man on a fresh horse, I was fading fast. My eyelids drooped; my lines of charactery symbols, normally straight as a privy path, began to wander. I glanced at the watch that lay on the desk. It was past midnight.

Mr. Shakespeare seemed to notice neither the lateness of the hour nor my nodding head, so caught up in his creation was he. I pinched my leg mercilessly, to jar myself into wakefulness. Now that he was racing along at last, it would not be fair of me to bring him up short by pleading exhaustion. I kept up as best I could until, finally, he began to stumble and came to a halt.

"End of Act Two," he said with satisfaction. "A fair night's work."

"Fair?" I said, and yawned widely. "I doubt whether I could survive a *good* night's work, then." I looked about at the papers I had strewn this way and that in my haste.

"Go on to bed," said Mr. Shakespeare. "I'll clean up here. Did I work you too hard?"

"Oh, Lord, sir," I said, and we shared a final, fatigued laugh.

When I stretched out on my mattress in our sleeping room, Sam stirred and murmured, "How did it go?"

"Like the wheel of Fortune," I said. "Now up, now down."

"I don't see why he agonizes so over it. After all, it's only a play."

For a change, the room was not filled with Jack's snoring. "What's happened to Jack?" I whispered to Sam.

Jack's grumpy voice replied from the darkness, "You're keeping me awake with all your gabbling, that's what."

"Sorry."

After a moment, I heard Jack's voice again. "I know what you're up to," he said.

"How do you mean?" I asked.

"With all your extra work. You're trying to get in good with the sharers, so they'll keep you on."

I made no reply to this. In fact I said nothing until I heard him begin to snore. Then I poked Sam.

"What?"

"Jack says I'm trying to get in good wi' the sharers so they'll keep me on. Do you suppose there's some chance they *won't*?"

"Why wouldn't they?"

"Well, we're making no money at all. An this keeps up, perhaps they'll ha' to let some of us go."

"Who would they have to play girls' parts, then?"

"Sal Pavy, for one."

"Ahh, you're far better than he is."

"How do you ken?" I said. "You've not seen him perform yet."

"Ha! I see him perform every day for the sharers, in the role of the Good Prentice."

"Aye, and they seem to find him very convincing."

"Then perhaps it's our duty to enlighten them."

"Nay, it's not," I said. "Whatever his faults he's one of us."

Sam laughed ironically. "Just don't try to tell *him* that."

Sal Pavy soon had the chance to show the rest of the company how capable an actor he was. To our great relief, we were welcomed by the mayor of Newark. He did question us closely, though, to be sure none of the company had any symptoms of the plague. Though the contagion had not yet reached his town, rumors of it had.

In London, when we were to perform for the Queen, we first had to present our play to her Master of Revels. Here, though our audience would be nothing like royalty, we were expected to play first for the mayor and his aldermen, who would then pass judgment on whether or not we were fit for public consumption.

Since we had failed in our attempt to perform *Love's Labour's Lost* in Newbury, the sharers determined to do it now, assuming that a provincial audience would prefer comedy to tragedy. Perhaps, I thought, recalling what

Mr. Shakespeare had said about the Queen's taste, they were not so different from royalty after all.

We were all of us a bit rusty from not having exercised our skills for so long, but once the play was under way we performed smoothly enough. Sal Pavy's early-morning practices served him well; so did his naturally haughty manner. It was difficult for me to watch him play the Princess of France or to act alongside him. In truth, I suppose I was resentful, for always before, Sander had been the one to play the Princess. But even I had to admit that Sal Pavy brought to the role an uncommon dignity and grace.

After the performance, he had praise heaped upon him by the sharers. Sam and I, not wishing to seem poor sports, said a few complimentary and wholly unconvincing words. The mayor and his friends were enthusiastic, too, and a public performance was set for the following afternoon. Again, we prentices were given a sheaf of handbills to scatter through the town.

We split up, to make the task go more quickly. As I was returning to our inn, I spotted a troupe of a dozen or so men, some on horseback and some afoot, approaching on the highway. When they drew nearer, I noticed that they wore brown cloaks and orange caps—the livery of Lord Pembroke's Men.

I had seen Pembroke's company perform at the Swan, but not often enough so I could recognize the individual players, particularly without their makeup. One of their number—a stout fellow of perhaps twenty, with a ruddy complexion and a generous belly—did look somehow familiar at first, but as he drew nearer I saw that he wore a leather patch over his right eye. I didn't recall ever encountering anyone with such a distinctive feature.

I hurried to the inn, ran upstairs, and burst into Mr. Armin's room. He looked up in surprise from a sheet of paper he had filled with his neat, elegant script. "Remind me to add to your other instruction a class in courtesy," he said.

"I'm sorry," I said breathlessly, "but I thought you'd want to ken."

"Ken what?"

"The Earl of Pembroke's Men are coming."

He set paper and pen aside and rose. "Are you certain?"

"I recognized their livery—brown cloaks, orange caps."

"Shrew them! They've had the same idea we did, it seems. I didn't foresee having to compete with another London company."

"But we're here first. They'll have to be content wi' the leavings, will they not?"

Mr. Armin played idly with the handle of the dagger he always wore at his belt. "Perhaps," he said thoughtfully. Then he looked up and smiled slightly at me. "Thanks for the warning, at any rate. Next time knock, though."

"Aye. I will." I glanced at the sheet of paper. "Are you writing a letter home?"

"That? No, no. It's a—" He paused, as though unsure whether or not to go on. "Just between us, it's a play."

"Truly? I didn't ken you were a playwright."

"I'm not much of a one. Not of the same rank as Will,

certainly. I'm revising an old work of mine called *Fool Upon Fool, or A Nest of Ninnies.* I thought something mindless might appeal more to these Yorkshire wights. No offense. I'm Yorkshire born and bred meself, as you ken," he said, lapsing into the speech of the region. "I can't say I'm thrilled to be back. What about you?"

I shrugged. "It's nothing to me one way or the other. If there's time, though, I'd like to visit th' orphanage in York where I spent me early years."

"We'll make time," said Mr. Armin. "For now, let's go and see what Pembroke's Men are up to."

But it seemed that our rivals had not taken rooms at our inn, for we saw no sign of them, nor had the other members of the company. "P-perhaps they've no money for b-bed and b-board," said Mr. Heminges with concern in his voice.

"They did appear somewhat shabby," I said. "They had no carewares and no trunks, only packs slung over their saddles."

"My guess," said Will Sly, "is that they've been forced to sell or to pawn some of their gear. They may have to change their name to Pem's Broke Men."

"We ought to keep an eye on our own equipment, then," put in Jack.

"Oh, I hardly think they'd stoop t-to stealing," said Mr. Heminges. "They're a reputable c-company, after all."

"Well, if they do," said Sam, "Sally will surely stop 'em." This brought a laugh from some of the others and a kick under the table from me.

If we could have seen a few hours into the future, no one would have found Sam's jest the least amusing. Sometime after midnight, the door to our sleeping room burst open and a voice shocked us from our sleep with a single word: "Fire!"

I sat upright, rubbing at my eyes. Mr. Armin was stalking about among us, shaking the sleepers roughly. "Get up! The wagons are afire! Come! There's no time to dress!" He flung open the door that led to the gallery and ran outside. The hired men and prentices staggered after him, half asleep still, barefoot and clad only in our nightshirts.

We had brought the carewares into the inn yard and pulled them alongside the stable, assuming they would be safe there. We were wrong. The fronts of both wagon boxes were ablaze, and the flames were climbing the sides, threatening to set the canvas tops alight. In their flickering light, I spotted Sal Pavy shuffling across the inn yard, straining at the weight of a leather water bucket whose contents spilled onto the cobbles and onto the hem of his nightshirt.

Stunned, I stood clutching the railing of the gallery for a moment. "Gog's blood!" I heard Jack cry as he rushed past me. "Pembroke's Men are trying to burn us out!" Then Will Sly yanked at my nightshirt, setting me in motion. As I scrambled down the stairs, a splinter jammed into one bare foot, but I ran on.

Sal Pavy tossed what little remained of his bucket of water ineffectually at the burning wagon. Mr. Armin took the bucket from him and handed it to Jack. "Fill it at the horse trough! The rest of you, take hold of the wagon tongues! We've got to get them away from the stable! Widge! See if you can pull those canvas tops off!"

While the men hauled at one careware, trying to get it rolling, I clambered aboard the other and, clinging to the high wooden side, began fumbling with the loops of rope that held the canvas in place. "All together—heave!" shouted Mr. Armin, and their wagon lurched into mine, nearly dislodging me. My bare foot struck someone on the pate. I glanced down to see that it was Mr. Shakespeare, straining with his good arm at the spokes of one of the wheels.

I pulled the last of the ropes free, flung the canvas aside, out of the reach of the flames, and sprang for the other careware. I was too late. The canvas top on it was already burning. I believe we would have lost our battle with the flames had we not at that moment received reinforcements in the form of the innkeeper and his ostler. With their help, our men got the careware moving and pushed it across the cobbles to the horse trough.

While Jack and Sam and I doused the fire with bucket after bucket of water—Sal Pavy seemed to have disappeared—the rest of the men returned for the other careware. Within minutes, both fires were out. The players dragged our costume and property trunks from the wagon beds. Even in the pale light from the innkeeper's lantern, I could see that the wood was badly charred and, of course, soaked with water.

We carried the trunks into the stable and inspected their

contents. The armor and weapons and other properties were mostly undamaged, but the top layer of clothing was scorched, and all of it was wet. We spread the garments on the hay in the loft to dry and, leaving Jack and Will Sly to guard them, retired to our beds, grateful that our bedding, at least, had not been in the wagons.

We found Ned Shakespeare still in the room and still sound asleep. "The devil take him!" muttered Sam. "He's slept through the whole thing!"

"Mr. Shakespeare will be furious. Perhaps we'd best not tell him. 'A may not have noticed." But as I said this, I caught a movement in the corner of my eye and turned to see Mr. Shakespeare standing in the doorway. He clearly saw his brother's sleeping form, but he said nothing, only shook his head as though he had expected nothing more, and turned away.

After we washed up, I got Sam to draw the splinter—or at least most of it—from my foot. "How do you suppose the fire began?" he asked me.

"Mr. Armin said it looked as though someone had dropped burning bundles of straw into the front of the wagon beds."

"Who would do such a thing, and why?"

"Someone who dislikes players, I'd say. A fanatical Puritan, perhaps."

"Or maybe Jack was right. Maybe it was Pembroke's Men, trying to get rid of the competition."

After the night's exertions, we were all—with the exception of Ned and Sal Pavy—cross and tired the next day. Mr.

Phillips and Jack had suffered superficial burns. To my surprise, they came to me—grudgingly, in Jack's case—for medical advice. The best I could do for them was to smear on a salve of tallow mixed with comfrey, but it seemed to give them some relief.

Despite everything, we managed a passable performance that afternoon and took in a respectable box—most of which we promptly laid out again to have the damaged costumes repaired. The town councillors profited as much as we did, or more, for they had men passing through the crowd hawking bottles of ale.

As we stood behind the curtain waiting to go on, Sal Pavy, in his guise as the Princess, surveyed my dress, which was less elegant than the one I usually wore when playing Rosaline. "Why are you wearing *that*?" he asked distastefully.

"Because me better one has half the skirt burned away." This dress, too, had an unpleasant smoky odor to it, as did Sam's. Sal Pavy's costume had escaped the conflagration; dandy that he was, he had taken it from the trunk beforehand and hung it in the stable to air out.

"Well, you look more like a milkmaid than a maid in waiting," he said. I let his remark pass, but I suspected Sam would not, and I was right.

"Did you know you've a hole there?" Sam said innocently.

"Where?" Sal Pavy demanded, twisting his head around and feeling the fabric at his rear with both hands.

"Right in the middle of your bum!" Sam said, and went

into a fit of laughter that, though he muffled it with one hand, I was sure could be heard out front. Sal Pavy flushed angrily and, hiking up his skirts, stalked off—a short stalk, as the area behind the curtain was but one pace in depth and perhaps ten from side to side. "Oh, my," said Sam. "I've offended Her Majesty."

Halfway through the play, I caught a glimpse of one of Pembroke's Men, the paunchy fellow with the eye patch, standing just inside the door of the hall, watching the proceedings soberly—not like one who has come to enjoy himself but like one who is sizing up the competition. Somehow I suspected he had not bothered to pay his penny.

We could not depart the following day until the town's tailors had our costumes ready, and so we got only as far as Southwell before night fell. Though it was a far smaller town than Newark, the sharers decided to try a performance there, in the only enclosed space that was large enough—the wool market. Despite the stench, we drew an enthusiastic crowd that must have comprised two-thirds of the local population.

Buoyed by our success, we went on to perform in Mansfield, Sheffield, and Doncaster, where we were equally well received. By the time we reached York, we were ahead enough so that Mr. Heminges could pay the hired men six shillings apiece, and the prentices three—our regular weekly wage. But we had been on the road for nearly a month now, and these were the first wages we had seen. Still, it was certainly better than nothing.

I had hoped the company might send a share of our earnings home to Mr. Pope and Sander, but Mr. Heminges did not feel we could spare any yet. Mr. Burbage, he assured me, would see that they and the boys were provided for. All the same, upon our arrival at the Black Swan in York, I wrote a letter to Sander at once and enclosed a shilling to buy treats for the boys and Tetty.

Because we had changed our route, no letter from London had reached us yet. The sharers had by now a firmer notion of where our travels were likely to take us. Once we left York, we were to turn southwest and make a long loop that would take us through Leeds, Manchester, Chester, Shrewsbury, Coventry, and Mr. Shakespeare's home town of Stratford before we returned to London. I wrote out this itinerary for Sander, hoping he might send a reply in care of one of the towns along our route.

The sharers had expressed concern that, with the slow progress we'd made since leaving Newark, Pembroke's Men or some other company might have preceded us. We were gratified to learn that no London troupe had played here in years, only a few companies of lesser stature who hailed from the northern shires.

The city fathers examined our papers carefully and, satisfied that we were a renowned and reputable company, engaged us to play the Merchant Adventurers' Hall for an entire week. In addition, we were to receive our remuneration not from the audience but from the city treasury, to the tune of thirty shillings per performance.

At the inn that evening we celebrated our good fortune

with generous rounds of ale. Mr. Shakespeare even took a night off from struggling with *Love's Labour's Won*, for which I cannot say I was sorry. Despite the title, I had begun to wonder whether we would indeed win out as a result of all our labors, or whether the play would at some point simply fizzle out, like a firework with a faulty fuse.

Sal Pavy, wearing his cheerful face, condescended to join us in our festivities for a time. Before he retired to his stable I saw him draw Mr. Armin aside and engage him in a conversation that, from their expressions, appeared to be a serious one.

When we had drunk all we could hold—the ale they served us prentices was, of course, watered down, or my head could not have stood much of it—and were making for our beds, Mr. Armin beckoned to me. I stepped into his room. "I want your thoughts on something," he said.

I smiled amiably, in a mood to grant anyone anything. "Some ailment, no doubt," I said, and hiccoughed. "I seem to have become the company's unofficial physician—ah, there's a tongue twister you can use, sir, in our elocution lessons. Say it three times rapidly: unofficial physician, unafishy physician, unofficial position. I am most efficient in my unofficial position as a fisherman's physician."

Mr. Armin patted my shoulder lightly, but it was enough to unbalance me, and I sat down abruptly. "You've had too much ale," he said.

"Aye," I said, "that's me *ale-ment.*"

"Perhaps we should discuss this tomorrow."

"Nay, nay, I'm all right. What is 't? An upset stomach? A sore throat?"

"I'm not looking for medical advice. It's a theatre matter. Sal Pavy has asked that, when we do *Titus Andronicus*, he be given the part of Lavinia."

I blinked, taken aback. "But—but that's *me* part."

"I know. But you've been so busy helping Mr. Shakespeare, I thought you might be happy to have one less responsibility."

"So you promised it to him?"

"No. I told him I'd discuss it with you."

"Oh," I said. Though I tried not to show it, I was hurt by the proposal, for it implied that I could readily be replaced. I did not wish to seem temperamental, or unreasonable, but neither did I care to give up one of my best parts, especially to Sal Pavy. "Does 'a ken the part?"

Mr. Armin nodded. "He's been studying it."

So that was what he'd been up to in those early-morning solo sessions. I wondered what other parts he'd been committing to memory. Feeling as though I'd been wronged, I said sullenly, "An you think 'a can do it better, then I yield to him."

"Widge. It's not a question of who does it better, you know that. Sal feels we're not using him enough, that's all."

"Then let *him* play doctor and take dictation," I replied heatedly. Then I slumped forward and wearily hung my head. "I'm sorry. I didn't mean that. I'm tired and I've drunk too much."

"I know. I should not have brought this up now. Go on to bed. We'll take it up at a more opportune time."

I rose and walked unsteadily to the door. "Nay," I said with forced nonchalance, "an 'a wants the part, 'a may ha' 't. I've no claim on 't."

We were scheduled to play *Titus Andronicus* on Wednesday afternoon; as I now had no need to review my lines, I asked for that morning off, and Mr. Armin granted it. Sam begged to come with me, but I put him off. A journey into one's past must be made alone.

The orphanage was even more dismal than I had remembered it. The squat, square stone building had once been a prison, and, though the bars had been removed from the narrow windows and from the doorways and the interior walls had been whitewashed, there was no getting rid of the air of gloom that pervaded the place.

A clamor of children's voices came from the big room that served as classroom and dining hall, and it sounded so like always that I fancied for a moment I truly had gone back in time—until I saw the figure coming toward me down the hall. At first I did not recognize her, so changed was she. In my memory, she was a vigorous, imposing woman with a voice that any player would have envied. The eight years that had passed since I left the orphanage to apprentice to Dr. Bright had not been kind to her. She was still rotund as always, but no longer robust. Her hair had gone gray, and the spring had gone from her step.

"Mistress MacGregor?" I said uncertainly.

"Aye," she replied. "What is it?"

"You may not recall me," I said. "I'm Widge."

Her worn face brightened. "Not recall you? I should say I can!" To my surprise she put her arms about me and kissed both my cheeks, then stepped back to look me over, still gripping my arms. "You've grown!" she exclaimed, and then laughed. "Of course, 'twould be a wonder if you had not!"

I smiled. This was the Mistress MacGregor I remembered. "Well," I said, embarrassed, "I've not grown nearly as much as I'd like. I'm a player now, you know."

"Are you indeed?" she said enthusiastically. "A player? And what might that be?"

"You ken—an actor. In plays. In London."

She put a hand to her mouth in astonishment. "You're never!"

"Aye. And wi' the Lord Chamberlain's men, too. We're playing here in York this week, an you'd care to come."

She looked dubious. "Would a person have to dress up fine-like?"

"Oh, nay. Only th' actors."

"Then I'll do it, if I can get away." She squeezed my arm tightly. "Losh, I'm so happy to see you and to hear you've made something of yourself. Not that I ever doubted it."

"Do you ken what's become of th' other boys?"

She shook her head sadly. "The plague claimed many of them. Och, for a time this place was more like a pesthouse than an orphanage. Those who lived through it and left standing up seldom care to come back again."

I felt a painful pang of guilt. For some reason—or perhaps for none at all—Fortune had seen to it that I escaped the city before the plague struck in 1594.

"Have you been to see your old master . . . I dinna mind his name."

"Dr. Bright."

"Aye, that's him. I always thought it a poor name for him; he did not seem verra bright to me." She threw up her hands and exclaimed, "Och, bless me! Had his name not come up, I'd have forgotten, sure as sure. I've something for you."

"You ha'?"

"Aye." She led me into her office—not by the ear, for a change. "I'd have sent it to you, but you'd gone from Dr. Bright's and he could not, or would not, say where." With one of the jangling keys at her waist, she opened the top of a battered desk and fished some object from one of the compartments inside.

When she placed it in my hand, I saw that it was an ornate crucifix on a delicate chain. The figure of Christ was carved from ivory and set into a gold filigreed cross. I glanced up at Mistress MacGregor, bewildered. "What . . . why . . . ?"

"Bide a bit," she said, "and I'll tell you." Obediently I took a seat on a rickety stool, feeling seven again and about to be chastised for my misbehavior. Mistress MacGregor sat at the desk and went on.

"About a year ago, I was summoned to the poorhouse, to the bedside of a dying woman named Polly—not a resident of the poorhouse, you ken, but a housekeeper there."

I nodded, wondering where this could be leading.

"I kenned the woman but little, so I was surprised that she should ask for me in her last hours. I was even more surprised when she took that crucifix from a table beside the bed and pressed it into my hand. 'What's this, then?' says I, and she says, so low I could scarcely hear her, she says, 'I done a bad thing and I want to make amends.' 'Well,' says I, 'perhaps I should fetch a priest, then.' 'Nay,' says she, 'only you can help,' and she points to that crucifix. 'I took that off a woman as died in childbirth, years ago. I kenned 'twas wrong to do it, but I liked the look of it, and I told meself she'd have no use for it any longer. I've regretted it ever since,' she says. 'I couldn't even bring meself to wear it ever, or to tell anyone what I'd done.' 'Why tell me, then?' says I. 'Because,' says she, 'you ken who it rightly belongs to, for the child she bore was given over to you.' "

I waited for Mistress MacGregor to go on. Instead she gazed expectantly at me, as a player will at another whose turn it is to speak. Then the import of what she had said struck me so soundly that I seemed suddenly unable to catch my breath. Finally, I managed to respond. "You mean to say that . . . that the child was me? But—but how can you be sure? You must have taken in dozens of orphans whose mothers died in the poorhouse."

"Aye, but—" She tapped the worn record book that lay open on her desk. "I've checked me records for that year—

it was the year that Polly was first hired on at the poor-house—and there were only two such cases. And in only one of them did the mother die afore she could even give the bairn a name."

The room fell silent save for the ticking of a clock on the mantel and the far-off sound of children's voices. I felt curiously displaced, detached and dreamlike, much the way I felt when I was playing a role upon the stage. With fingers that seemed not to belong to me I turned the crucifix over in my palm. On the reverse side someone had scratched some words, doubtless with the point of a knife. I had to wipe my eyes on my sleeve before I could make them out: FOR SARAH.

"Was that . . . was that her name, then? Sarah?"

"Aye. That was your mother."

"Me mother." I whispered the words, trying them out upon my tongue. "Me mother. After all this time." I raised my eyes beseechingly to Mistress MacGregor. "Did this Polly tell you aught about her, then? What she was like? What she looked like, even?"

Mistress MacGregor shook her head regretfully. "When they found your mother on the doorstep, she was near dead already; apparently she never spoke a single word. I had no chance to question Polly any further; not long after she gave me that cross, she drew her last paiching breath—without even being shriven by a priest." Mistress MacGregor learned toward me, as though to disclose some dire secret. "She was a Catholic."

"Me mother?" I said.

"Nay, I meant Polly. Though for all I ken your mother was as well. They're the ones as go in for the fancy crosses, mostly."

"A Catholic," I said. I knew little about Catholics, save that the Queen did not like them. Our enemy, Spain, was, after all, peopled by Catholics. So far as I knew, I had never met a Catholic. But then an allegiance to the Old Church was not, I gathered, the sort of thing one would confess at the drop of a hat.

"I only say she may have been. I canna say for certain. I did ask the other folk at the poorhouse if they minded your mother, but none had worked there more than a few years. I went through their records for that month and year, too, but they told me nothing, not even her name."

"Would there not be a grave?" I asked.

"Aye, but 'twould be a pauper's grave, all unmarked. I'm sorry."

I felt a pain in my hand, and realized I had been gripping the crucifix so tightly that Christ's crown of thorns had pierced my palm. I stared down at the drops of blood that welled from the wound and wondered if my mother, too, had clutched this cross for comfort as she lay dying—and giving birth to me. I wiped the crucifix on my breeches; traces of the blood remained in the deep scratches that made up her name. It was a pity that whoever had engraved the message had not seen fit to add her surname. It would have given me a stronger clue to her identity—and, after fifteen years of being known only as Widge, I would have had a real name at last, or half a one, at any rate.

"An she was a local lass," said Mistress MacGregor, "there must be someone here who kenned her."

"Aye," I said, a dell of hope rising up within me. "That's so. There must be someone who would recognize this cross, if I but kenned where to look."

"Well . . . an she did belong to the Old Church, then you might seek out others of that faith. Folk do say they stick together." She leaned forward again, with one hand alongside her mouth, for all the world like an actor signaling that he is about to reveal something slightly scandalous. "They also say that the Catholics are fonder of their drink than most. If I was you, I'd begin looking in the taverns."

The town's drinking establishments were easy enough to find. Whereas a tavern in London could be identified by the ivy or red lattice by its entrance, here in the north the sure sign was a large painted hand made of wood, projecting on a pole from the window. I started with the Hog's Head in Coney Street. No one in the place found the crucifix familiar, and the only Sarah any of them knew was a lady of ill repute who was very much alive. The story was the same at the next tavern and the next.

As I emerged from the Raven, I glanced at the clock on the steeple of the town hall. The afternoon's performance was but a little over an hour away, and I was expected to lend a hand with prompting and costume changes and the like. I dared not shirk my duties, lest the sharers decide they could do without me altogether.

I had begun to suspect that my quest was a hopeless one.

Still, I reasoned, it could do no harm to ask about in one or two more taverns, so I walked on to an unnamed alehouse that occupied the ground floor of a run-down house. Folk sometimes call the main room of a tippling house the "dark parlor"; this one certainly lived up to its name. It was so dim within that I had to stand inside the entrance for several minutes before I could see properly.

The benches that flanked the half-dozen trestle tables were mostly empty; clearly this was not one of the city's more popular drinking spots. I could see why. The rushes on the floor looked as though they'd not been changed since the Queen took the throne; the tops of the tables were chipped and gouged from years of being used as a sticking place for daggers; and the chinks in the wood had filled in with a putty composed of food remnants and dried-up puddles of ale.

The few patrons in the place turned hostile stares upon me, as did the tavern keeper, who was emerging from the taproom with a pint mug in each hand, the contents slopping over rims. "Good afternoon," I ventured. He gave me not so much as a nod in reply. I approached him, dangling the crucifix before me like some talisman to ward off danger. "I wonder if you've ever seen a cross of this sort before."

The tippler gave it a cursory glance, shook his head brusquely, and plunked the mugs down before his paltry pair of customers. One of them was a small, gnomelike fellow with but half an ear on one side—the rest of it had, I suspected, been clipped off as a punishment for thieving. He reached out one grimy hand and drew the crucifix nearer, to squint at it with rheumy eyes. Then he, too, shook his head and retreated with his drink into the dark recesses of the alehouse.

I tried to show the cross to the second man, but he waved me off. With a sigh, I sat down on the end of a bench, meaning to rest a few moments before heading back to our inn. "An you don't drink," said the tippler, "you don't sit."

I would, in truth, have welcomed a pint of ale, for I'd had neither drink nor food since early in the day. But I had only two shillings to my name and no notion of how long they'd have to last me. In any case, I would have been reluctant to drink a drop from any vessel in this unsanitary place.

Wearily, I got to my feet and headed for the door. Just as my hand fell upon the latch, a commanding voice from the gloomy depths at the rear of the room called out, as sharp and sudden as a cannon shot, "Hold!"

I was accustomed to doing as I was bid. I stopped in my tracks. "Come here, boy!" ordered the voice.

I turned slowly. "Me?"

"Of course, you. Do you see any other boys about?"

I moved hesitantly toward the rear of the room. The wight with half an ear sat at a table there, but I did not think his was the voice that had called me. "Come, come," said the voice, more kindly. "I'll not bite you." It came from a figure sitting in a dark alcove formed where the fireplace jutted into the room. "Sit down," the man said, and gestured to a bench that faced the fireplace. Once more I did as I was told. "Roger!" called the man, whose face I still could not see clearly. "A pint of ale for my young friend, if you please."

"Who's going to pay for 't?" asked the tippler.

"Ah, Roger," said the man reproachfully, "you know I'm good for it."

"I can't pay me bills wi' promises," grumbled the tippler, but he brought the pint all the same and thrust it into my hands.

"Fair 'chieve you," said the stranger, and clinked his mug against mine. "Drink up."

Obediently I put the earthenware mug to my mouth and did my best to drink without actually touching my lips to the vessel. Over its rim I studied my drinking companion as well as I could, given the little light that reached into the alcove.

The first thing that struck me about him was that he did not seem to belong here, in these shabby surroundings. Unlike the other patrons of the place, whose tattered and soiled tunics marked them as members of the laboring class—or, more likely, the thieving class—this fellow wore a gentleman's attire, a doublet and breeches that were, if not exactly new or stylish, at least presentable.

He leaned forward and, with a pair of tongs, fished a glowing ember from a clay pot on the hearth to light his long-stemmed clay pipe, giving me a better look at his features. He was about of an age with Mr. Shakespeare and Mr. Burbage—that is, thirty-five or so. His ginger-colored hair was unusually close-cropped. With the exception of Sal Pavy we prentices wore our hair short, finding it more convenient and comfortable when we donned the wigs that transformed us into women. But this man's hair was shorter still, and his beard was trimmed to within a quarter inch of his face. His long nose showed definite signs of having been broken, perhaps more than once. These features, plus his rather stiff-backed posture, put me in mind of a military man and, as I shortly learned, I had read him right.

The man puffed on his pipe and blew forth a billow of tobacco smoke that choked me. He laughed. "They say this weed is beneficial to the lungs—once you get used to it." After another few puffs, he added, "Forgive me for being so abrupt with you a moment ago. I was once a soldier, and have not yet lost the old habit of ordering folk about."

"What do you want?" I asked, impatient to be off to the Merchant Adventurers' Hall.

"I overheard you asking the others about a certain cross, and it piqued my curiosity." His speech, too, was more like that of a gentleman than of an ordinary workingman, and bore little trace of Yorkshire. "Might I have a look at it?"

I drew the crucifix from my wallet and held it by the chain before him. He bent forward, a bit awkwardly, as though the movement pained him, and laid the cross on his palm. I heard a sharp intake of breath, then he said softly, "By my fay! It's the very same!"

117

"Wh-what do you mean?" I asked, my voice suddenly shaky. "Do you recognize this?"

He let the cross go and glanced up at me, his eyes wide, their pupils like dark pools without a bottom. "Recognize it?" he said. "It's mine—or once was."

"Yours? Nay! How can that be? It belonged to me mother!"

He stared at me for a moment, with an expression I could not read. "It was I who gave it to her, and it was I who engraved the message on the back."

"The—the message?"

He nodded. " 'For Sarah.' "

I was stunned. He had not turned the cross over and, even had he done so, he could not have read the faint letters in this dim light. It took me a moment to respond. "You kenned her, then?"

He gave a small, rather rueful smile. "Better than anyone, I think. We would have wed, had not her family stood in our way." Again he took up the crucifix, which was twisting slowly about as it dangled from my trembling hand, and gently traced the ornate design with one finger, as though looking at it called up my mother's face. "My family were Catholics, hers Protestants. Though they forbade her to see me, we carried on a courtship for many months, at night, in secret. I would have wed her in secret, too, but she could not bring herself to defy her parents that far. So . . . " He shrugged. "So I became a soldier and went off to Ulster to fight Tyrone. When I returned from Ireland, I could find no trace of her or her family. Eventually I learned that her parents had died of the plague. I could only assume that she had met the same fate."

"Nay, she did not," I whispered. "She died i' the poorhouse . . . after giving birth to me."

When I was a child in the orphanage, I was convinced, like many of my fellow orphans, that a mistake had been made, that I had only been separated somehow from my mother and father. I felt certain that one day they would come for me, and I imagined our tearful reunion so clearly that it seemed inconceivable it would not come to pass.

Now, at last, it had, and it was nothing like I had imagined. We did not cry, we did not embrace, we did not even speak for some time. We only sat in silence, linked by the cross in his hand and the chain in mine. Finally he sat back, took a deep draught from his mug, and wiped his mouth. "Well. I don't often find myself at a loss for words." He laughed uncertainly and spread his hands. "What do we do now, then? Introduce ourselves?"

I gave a weak and awkward laugh as well. "It would be a start, I suppose."

He held out a large hand with short, broad fingers. "I'm Jamie Redshaw, lately of Her Majesty's musketeers."

Like an actor playing his part by rote I reached out and shook his hand. "And I'm Widge. Or at least that's what they call me. Me mother didn't live long enough to give me a proper name."

"I'm sorry," he said. "I didn't know. I didn't know what had become of her. I didn't even know she was with child. My child." He took another long drink, then sat gazing at me over the rim of his mug, appraising me as I had earlier been appraising him. "You must be thirteen or fourteen, then."

"Fifteen," I said.

He shook his head and ran a hand through his bristly hair. "It's been that long? It's difficult to believe. You've spent all those years here, in the orphanage?"

"Nay, I was apprenticed to Dr. Bright of Berwick for a time, then I went to London, and for the past year I've been a prentice wi' the Lord Chamberlain's Men."

He raised his eyebrows. "The Chamberlain's Men, is it? You've done well for yourself."

"You ken the company?"

"Of course. I saw them perform *Twelfth Night* only yesterday. I don't recall seeing you, though."

"Well, I looked rather different in me wig and makeup." I gasped then, and leaped to my feet. "Oh, gis! I nearly forgot! They'll be starting the performance! I ha' to leave!" I turned toward the door, then turned abruptly back again. "But—but I can't leave! There's so much . . . We haven't even . . . " I waved my hands in frustration, torn between my duty to the company and my desire to learn everything at once about a mother and father who had so suddenly and unexpectedly materialized.

Laughing, Jamie Redshaw rose to his feet and clapped me on the back, so soundly that it stung. "Don't fret, Widge. I'm not going to disappear. Why don't I come with you, and we can talk further after the performance."

"Oh, aye!" I said gratefully, and we made for the door.

"You've not paid for your drinks!" the scowling tippler reminded us.

Jamie Redshaw waved to him as blithely as though the man had wished us good fortune. "In due time, Roger. All in due time."

As we headed for the Merchant Adventurers' Hall, I glanced furtively at Jamie Redshaw again and again, trying to get my mind around the notion that this was my father walking next to me. It was difficult. As far as I could tell, our looks were as unlike as could be. My hair was dark; his was fair. My eyes were blue, his brown. My frame was small and slight; his was large and stout.

My mind was a mingle-mangle of thoughts and questions, each fighting to be spoken first. Some I had been wondering about for years; others had occurred to me but a moment before. Some were so trivial and foolish that I thrust them aside; others were so difficult that I felt I dared not put them to him just yet.

I began with the ones that had been with me longest. "Can you . . . can you tell me what me mother looked like?"

At first I thought he had not heard me, for he looked lost in his thoughts, too. Finally he raised his head, gazed at me a long moment, and then said, "Like you."

"And what was her surname?"

He scratched his short beard thoughtfully. "Hmm. It's been a long time; give me a moment. Rogers, that's it."

"Has she no kin left here?"

He shook his head. "None. If she had, I would have found them."

"Would you?" I said, more bitterly than I meant to. "You failed to find me."

He turned to me with a look that was half angry, half reproachful. "I had no idea you existed," he said.

We walked on in silence. Despite the fact that I was a head shorter, I found myself having to slow my pace so as not to get ahead of him. He did not limp, exactly; he seemed merely to favor his left side a little, to hesitate slightly each time he brought his left leg forward. Though he carried an impressive hardwood walking stick with a carving of a snarling lion's head on the handle, he did not lean on it but walked along rigidly upright, swinging the stick at his side.

"I'm sorry to slow you down," he said. "I've a wound that gives me a twinge now and again."

"A sword wound?" I asked.

"No, a fragment of an Irish cannonball. It went through my hip, the surgeon told me, and lodged near the base of my spine."

"Gog's blood!" I breathed. "All I've ever done is mock

fighting on the stage. I can scarcely imagine what it's like to be in the thick of a real battle."

"I hope you never have to learn," said Jamie Redshaw soberly.

I hoped so, too. Yet I couldn't help feeling, for the first time, a trifle ashamed of my profession, and wondering what a man who had truly known death and tragedy would make of our pale imitations.

"It's very odd," I said, "that you should be a soldier."

He frowned slightly. "Why? What do I look as though I'd be? A plowman?"

"Nay, nay," I replied hastily. "I only meant it's odd because not long ago someone asked about me father and, on a whim, I said 'a was a soldier. Ha' you always been, or were you a prentice, like me?"

"I apprenticed to a boatwright."

"A boatwright? Not in Yorkshire, surely?"

Laughing, Jamie Redshaw held up his stick as though to ward off my onslaught of questions. "Patience, boy, patience! We can't hope to make up for fifteen years in as many minutes, you know! As I said, I'll not disappear. There will be plenty of opportunity later for all your questions. For now, let us simply get to know one another, as new-made acquaintances do, shall we?"

I nodded, embarrassed. "Aye. I'm sorry."

By the time we reached the Merchant Adventurers' Hall, a long stream of playgoers were paying their pennies to Sam, who had a gatherer's box suspended by a thong around his neck. "Where have you been?" he wanted to know. "Everyone's been asking me."

"I've been—I was—" It was all too much to try to explain. "I'll tell you later," I mumbled, and squeezed past the paying folk.

" 'Here!" Sam called after Jamie Redshaw. "You've got to pay your penny, sir!"

" 'A's wi' me, Sam," I told him.

"Who is he?" asked Sam, never one to hold back a question, however difficult.

I glanced uncertainly at Jamie Redshaw, who gave me a conspiratorial wink. "A new-made acquaintance," he said.

At one end of the hall, the city had erected a stage for us nearly as large as the one at the Globe. I led Jamie Redshaw around the curtain to where the players, already in costume, were making up one another's faces in the absence of a decent mirror.

"Sorry I'm late," I blurted, before anyone could take me to task for it. "It won't happen again, I promise."

"It's not l-like you," said Mr. Heminges. "We thought you m-must have good reason."

"Actually," said Will Sly, "we were taking wagers. Mr. Shakespeare fancied that your old master had kidnapped you. Jack was sure you'd deserted and gone back to London. My contention was that you'd spent all your salary on strong drink and were out cold in a tavern somewhere."

"Well, you're all wrong," I said, "though I was in several taverns."

"Aha!" cried Will triumphantly. "I was nearest the mark!"

"Who's your friend?" asked Mr. Armin. "A would-be player?"

"Nay, 'a's . . . " I hesitated. The notion of having a father at hand was still so unfamiliar to me.

"I'm Jamie Redshaw," he volunteered. "And you have a performance to do, so I'd best let you get on with it. Widge, we'll talk later." He stepped down from the platform and disappeared behind the curtain.

Alarmed, I ran after him. "You're not leaving?"

"No, no," he assured me. "I'll just be out front here, watching the play."

I nodded and backed away, keeping an eye on him as long as possible, fearful still that he might vanish and, with him, the only link I had to my heritage.

The company were all too busy to question me further. I helped make up faces and pin together splitting seams; I made certain all the properties were in their places; I retrieved from the script trunk the plot of the play, which showed all the actors' entrances, and hung it on the back side of the curtain. It was fortunate that I had done all these things a hundred times before, for my mind was not on them.

In between tasks, I stole a look out into the audience to make certain Jamie Redshaw was still there. When I could not spot him at once, my heart seemed to stop; then I caught sight of him off to one side, perched upon one of the stools that were reserved for those who could afford an extra sixpence.

Once the performance began, I volunteered to hold the book and throw lines out to those actors who were floundering. Though Sal Pavy had never before played the part of Lavinia on the stage, he showed no sign of needing help. On the few occasions when he did lose his way a little, he managed to get his bearings again with no prompting from me.

I wished now, more than ever, that I had not been so obliging as to let him have the part. I longed to make my father proud of me, and I could not do that from behind the stage. And yet perhaps it was just as well this way; considering the state my mind was in, I would likely have forgotten half my lines.

I did my best to pick out flaws in Sal Pavy's performance and did, indeed, find two. When he came on at the end of Act II with his hands lopped off, I could see the tips of his fingers poking out of one sleeve; and when he tripped over the hem of his dress in Act III, I distinctly heard him mutter a curse, despite the fact that his tongue was supposedly cut out.

But as far as acting ability was concerned, I had to admit—difficult as it was for me to do so—that he played the part, as theatre folk say, to the life. All trace of the spoiled and self-important Sal Pavy had vanished, and in his place was a piteous young woman who had been "ravished and wronged." When I had played Lavinia, and was called upon to scratch out the names of the villains in the dirt, holding the staff in my teeth and guiding it with my stumps, my clumsiness sometimes elicited laughter, not pity, from the audience. When Sal Pavy did the scene, there was not a single snicker, not a sound except perhaps a sniffle or two from some softhearted member of the audience. I could not help it; I disliked him more than ever.

True to his word, Jamie Redshaw rejoined us after the play was done and returned with us to the inn. Though the situation was an awkward one for me, I should have known how to conduct myself. I had, after all, had dozens of fathers before this—Leonato in *Much Ado*, Shylock in *The Merchant of Venice*, Polonius in *Hamlet*. Yet I had always been a daughter, never a son. I felt as though I were living out that dream every actor dreads, the one in which he is unexpectedly called upon to play a role totally unfamiliar to him. I had no notion of what to say, or where the day's developments might lead.

Happily, Jamie Redshaw seemed more sure of himself than I. Over dinner, he revealed to the company what he had implied to me. I had expected my fellow players to react with surprise to this revelation, and they did. I had also expected them to be delighted for me. I had, after all, after fifteen years of thinking myself an orphan, discovered that I had a family, or at least part of one.

They were cordial enough, to be sure, and offered their congratulations, but I sensed a certain reserve, especially on the part of Mr. Armin and Mr. Shakespeare, as though they were taking Jamie Redshaw's measure. It put me in mind of the way they behaved toward the players who auditioned for temporary roles at the Globe. I had the feeling they were debating whether or not he was suited to the part.

As for me, I was, I suppose, more like a playwright who has waited year upon year for some actor to audition for a crucial role in his play and gotten not a single prospect. I would likely have taken anyone who happened along.

Not that I was disappointed in the player I got. Watching Jamie Redshaw converse with the members of the company, I felt an unexpected and unfamiliar swell of something that I could only identify as pride. Though he was a simple soldier, a man of action, and not a scholar, he seemed quite comfortable in the company of men as intelligent and witty as the sharers. In fact, he behaved as if they were not new-made acquaintances but the oldest of friends. If he was discomfited at all by their appraising manner he did not show it; indeed, he seemed not to notice. He proceeded to give a highly entertaining—and highly exaggerated—account of how he and I had met. When he recounted how I fell off my stool in astonishment, it drew a round of raucous laughter. Though I did not recall doing such a thing, I did not spoil the hilarity by saying so.

In the midst of Jamie Redshaw's story the innkeeper approached us and cleared his throat. "Begging your pardon, sirs, but there's a wight outside says 'a desires to speak wi' someone in your company."

"Well, h-have him c-come in," said Mr. Heminges.

" 'A says 'a wishes to talk out there."

The sharers glanced at one another. Mr. Armin got to his feet. "I'll go see what it's about."

When he was gone, Jamie Redshaw resumed his story,

but was interrupted again by a sudden loud snoring sound close at hand. I turned to see that Sam had put his head down on the table and was fast asleep. Several of the company laughed, but I did not, for I had taken note of how flushed Sam's face looked and how the sweat stood out on his brow. "I hope 'a's not ill."

"J-just tired, I expect," said Mr. Heminges. "That g-gathering box is a heavy b-burden for a boy."

"Especially considering how much money we took in," added Mr. Phillips. "Why don't you help him up to bed, Widge?"

I hesitated, reluctant yet to let Jamie Redshaw out of my sight. Seeming to sense my dilemma, he smiled and nodded. "Go on. I'll still be here when you get back."

As I assisted Sam in mounting the stairs, I heard Jamie Redshaw take up the thread of his story again. I could not make out the words; whatever they were, they drew more appreciative laughter from his audience. When I returned to the main room of the inn, however, no one was laughing, and Jamie Redshaw was no longer holding forth. Everyone was silent and sober-faced. "What's wrong?" I asked.

Mr. Armin, who had taken his place again at the table, looked up at me. "Our stay here has been cut short."

"For what reason?" I cried. "Did they not like us?"

"I'm afraid we've been upstaged," replied Mr. Armin. "By the plague."

The man Mr. Armin had gone to speak with was the town's bailiff. His message was that, since our company's arrival in York, there had been a rash of plague deaths. No one was accusing us of having brought them on, but the local officials thought it best to ban any public gatherings for a time, until the threat died down.

We had scheduled a shortened version of *The Taming of the Shrew* for the following morning, and we would be permitted to proceed with it, but we were not to finish out the week. Every member of our company was upset by the news, for it meant only half the profit we had anticipated. I had even more cause for distress; I would have to leave behind my newfound father without ever having gotten to know him. I did have an alternative, of course. I could drop out of the company and remain in York. But that prospect was even more painful than the first.

"I'm sorry, Widge," said Mr. Armin. "I know this creates a dilemma for you."

"If you f-feel you need to stay a few m-more days," said Mr. Heminges, "we c-could manage without you, I suppose." Though I knew he meant only to ease my mind, his words stung me. I would have preferred to hear that I was indispensable, that the company could not possibly spare me.

"No," Jamie Redshaw put in unexpectedly. "It would not be fair to the company for Widge to stay on here. You're having to double up parts as it is." I stared at him in dismay. Now I was being betrayed by both sides. Why was he so ready to let me go? Did I mean nothing to him?

"B-but you've only j-just found one another. We've no w-wish to wrench him from you so s-soon."

"Nor do I wish you to," said Jamie Redshaw calmly. "Fortunately I have a solution that I think will suit everyone."

"You do?" I said.

Smiling, he spread his hands palms upward. "It's simple," he said. "I'll come with you."

After only a few minutes' discussion among themselves, the sharers agreed to Jamie Redshaw's proposal. Mr. Heminges made it clear that they could not afford to pay him a hired man's wages; but, like every prentice's father, he was entitled to two shillings a week from the company in return for his son's services.

"Well," said Jamie Redshaw amiably, "it's more than I'm

receiving at the moment. By rights, I should be collecting an army pension, but they continually deny me it."

"Why?" I asked.

There was more than a trace of bitterness in his laugh. "Because," he said, "they're the army."

Through the night I heard Sam thrashing about restlessly and, when I put my hand on him to still him, I felt that he was soaked with perspiration; though the air in the room was close and warm, it did not account for such a surfeit of sweat.

In the morning he was too weak to come down to breakfast, so I took him up a bowl of porridge. Once he'd gotten it down he seemed stronger and in better spirits. Even so, when we set out for the Merchant Adventurers' Hall, he seemed hardly able to keep himself upright. "Are you going to be able to go on?" I asked.

"I'll manage," he said, his voice hoarse.

"After the performance, I'll tell them you need to see a physician."

"The company can't afford that," he said. "Can't you give me something?"

"How can I? I don't ken what's wrong wi' you."

He stopped and put a hand that trembled slightly on my arm. Softly he said, "It's not the contagion, is it, Widge?"

"Nay," I said, trying to sound confident and trying, too, not to shrink back from his touch. "Nay, I'm sure it's just some fever or other."

I took Sam's place at the entrance, collecting the patrons' pennies. I had expected, after what we learned the night before, to see our audience dwindle drastically. But either the news of the plague deaths had not yet reached everyone's ears or else they had all determined to take in one last performance before the privilege was denied them, for folk were flocking to the theatre in greater numbers than ever.

The box grew so heavy with coins that I had to set it at my feet and collect the money in my hand—until I came to think that someone in the throng might, in passing their money to me, also be passing on the plague. I opened the lid of the box, then, and asked each one to drop his money in.

Sam, who was playing several small roles, held up somehow through the first three acts. But in Act IV, he came on as Biondello, spoke his line—"O master, master, I have watched so long that I am dog-weary"—and collapsed upon the boards. I froze, unable to think of how to thribble my way out of this.

But Sal Pavy, in his guise as Bianca, was quicker-witted. "Ah, sir," he said to Ned Shakespeare as Lucentio, "you work your men too hard by far"—a clever bit of improvised pentameter. Then he paraphrased Sam's lines, still in perfect meter: "I spy a person coming down the hill will serve the turn."

I had presence of mind enough to change my line— "What is he, Biondello?"—to "What is he, Mistress, pray?" Sal Pavy replied with Biondello's part. When he and Ned left the stage, they dragged Sam's limp form with them. The audience must have thought it was all in the script, for it fetched a laugh.

Though we revived Sam with tincture of myrrh, he was too weak to go on, so we worked around his absence. He still refused to see a physician. "All I need is to rest a while," he assured us. The sharers, wanting to push on to the next town where we might perform, had him ride atop our rolled-up bedding in the careware, and this time no one objected, not even Jack.

The pace of the procession was more brisk than usual and I could see that Jamie Redshaw, with his stiff gait, was finding it difficult to keep up with the carewares. "There's no need to tax yourself," I told him confidentially. "We'll catch up wi' them on the hills."

When we fell a bit behind the others, I said, "Did you take in the morning's performance, then?"

He nodded but offered nothing further.

"Well?" I prompted. "How did you like it?"

He cast me an amused glance. "I suppose what you mean is, how did I like you?"

I felt myself go red. "I did not want it to seem as though I were angling for compliments."

"You did well," he said. I waited for him to go on, but he said nothing more on the matter. I tried to dull the disappointment I felt by telling myself that, of course, being a soldier he had likely had little experience with the theatre and did not know what to say. But I had used that same sort of reasoning over and over to excuse his lack of fatherly affection toward me, and it was wearing thin.

It was well before dark when we spied the town of Harrogate ahead of us. We were spied in turn by a man—a merchant, from the look of him—approaching on horse-back. To my surprise, he at once wheeled his horse about and headed back toward town at a gallop.

"Now that's a bad sign," said Ned Shakespeare.

"Perhaps 'a merely forgot something," I suggested, "and had to go back for 't."

"Perhaps he's gone to get up a welcoming committee for us," said Jamie Redshaw.

We did indeed find a committee of a dozen or so men waiting for us, but they did not have a welcoming air about them. They stood blocking the road, their legs planted wide, their arms crossed, as though daring us to try and pass.

We pulled up the carewares, and Mr. Heminges and Mr. Armin rode forward to talk with the apparent leader of the group, a lanky man wearing the leather jerkin of a constable. The discussion appeared to be a heated one. Finally the blockade of bodies opened up and let our little troupe move on. The townsmen looked no more cordial than before, however, nor did they disperse. In fact they walked alongside us, as though escorting us.

Jamie Redshaw smiled in a friendly fashion and tried to exchange a few words with one of their number, but the man would not respond; he only stared straight ahead, with a scowl on his face. We came to an inn, but the sharers marched us on past it. We did not even pause until we were all the way through the town and into the countryside again. Then Mr. Heminges signaled us to halt, dismounted, and gathered us prentices and hired men about him.

"Why did they not let us stay?" demanded Ned Shakespeare.

"It's the contagion, isn't it?" I said.

He held up his hands to silence us. "P-please. G-give me a chance to tell you. We were p-preceded, it seems, by another troupe of p-players."

"Pembroke's Men!" cried Ned.

"No, apparently they were no legitimate c-company at all, only a company of thieves. They p-passed themselves off as players, of course. They'd had ill luck, they said, and asked the m-mayor for money for f-food and lodging, to be repaid out of the b-box from the next day's performance. They p-paid the innkeeper with promises as well, and then left in the m-morning with all the advance money and without g-giving a performance—save the one with which they d-duped the mayor. Naturally he was n-not anxious to be t-taken in again, by us."

"But we have papers!" protested Jack. "Did you show them our papers?"

"Of c-course. But these rogues had p-papers, too—very official looking, and very f-false."

"When were they here?" asked Jamie Redshaw.

"They left j-just this morning."

"Then we should not be wasting time," Jamie Redshaw declared, smacking his walking stick impatiently against his palm. "We've got to catch up with them."

Mr. Heminges smiled wryly. "We are not s-soldiers, Mr. Redshaw, looking to d-do battle with the enemy."

"But if we don't overtake them, they'll spoil every town for us before we get there!"

"I r-realize that," said Mr. Heminges, a trifle more sharply. "But we c-can assume they will stick to the smaller t-towns, where n-no one is likely to know the real P-Pembroke's Men. We'll t-try our luck in more p-populous places."

Jamie Redshaw shook his head disapprovingly. "Avoiding them will solve nothing. I'd confront them now, before they do more harm."

"Ah, but you see, you're n-not in charge of this c-company, Mr. Redshaw," said Mr. Heminges pointedly, and walked away.

I had watched the preceding scene with great discomfort. Though I felt my father's reasoning was sound and I wanted very much to ally myself with him, I was at the same time reluctant to speak out against the sharers.

While we were stopped, I got into our small stock of medicinal herbs and prepared for Sam an infusion of willow bark, a popular antidote for fever. But he no longer had a fever; he was trembling all over with chills. "How are you?" I asked as I covered him with my cloak.

"Oh, Lord, sir!" he said, and laughed shakily. Mr. Shakespeare's "answer to fit all questions" had by now become a familiar jest among the members of the company. "I heard what happened," he added. "Where will we go now?"

"Leeds, I expect. We should be there in a few hours, and then you'll have a proper bed."

"I'm all right," he murmured. "Don't fret about me."

Jamie Redshaw had taken advantage of the pause to light his pipe. As I jumped down from the careware, he asked, "How is your friend?"

"Not so good as I hoped, nor so bad as I feared." Softly, so Sam would not hear, I added, "Would that I could examine his legs for red marks; it would give me a better idea of what we're dealing wi'."

Jamie Redshaw puffed at his pipe a moment. "Whether or not it's the plague, you mean?"

"Aye. 'A's got his woolen hose on yet, from the play. An I ask him to remove them, 'a may guess that I'm looking for signs of the contagion. I've no wish to alarm him. It may be naught but the ague."

"He shows no other symptoms, then? No pustules?"

I shook my head. "Pray that 'a does not, for an 'a does, every one of us is in danger of being next."

Mr. Armin reined in his black mare and waited for us to come up alongside him. "This stretch of road between Harrogate and Leeds is a desolate one," he said, so all the hired men could hear. "Keep your weapons handy. No one is likely to try to rob a group of this size, but we can't be too careful."

"I ha' no weapon," I reminded him.

"How can you say that?" he replied in mock surprise. "Is the road not full of rocks?" He urged his mount on to the head of the procession again.

"Rocks?" said Jamie Redshaw.

"Aye," I said, embarrassed. "We had a skirmish back in

Newbury, and I pelted our attackers wi' stones. You'd think the company would trust me wi' a sword. I've been taking lessons in scriming for most of a year." Though I managed to sound resentful, secretly I was just as glad that no one expected me to exercise my sword-fighting skills except upon the stage. Sal Pavy, I noticed, had not called his lack of a weapon to anyone's attention. I glanced down at Jamie Redshaw's belt. "But . . . you've no weapon, either."

"Ah, that's where you're wrong." He shifted his walking stick to his left hand, gripped the carved lion's head in his right, and, in one swift sweeping motion, drew forth from the stick a thin blade two feet or more in length.

"That's clever," said Ned Shakespeare. "Where'd you come by that?"

"I won it in a game of primero."

Will Sly eyed the abbreviated blade. "I should hardly think it a match for a full-length weapon."

"Nor is it meant to be. It's the element of surprise that makes it effective."

"So, you're a fair hand at cards, then?" asked Ned.

"A bit better than fair, I should say."

Ned smiled slyly. "Shall we test your prowess when we reach our lodgings?"

Jamie Redshaw made an exaggerated bow. "At your service, sir. Presuming that we do, in fact, find lodgings."

As the afternoon waned, it began to look as if we might not. The sun approached the horizon, and still there was no habitation in sight, only vast stretches of deserted moorland on either side of the highway, dotted with clumps of furze. The only signs that any soul had ever passed this way before us were the wheel ruts, a few crumbling horse droppings, and a tilted, weathered stone cross beside the road, erected ages ago, I supposed, by some religious order to give comfort to weary travelers. Jack fumbled in his wallet for a penny and placed it atop the cross.

"What's that for?" asked Ned Shakespeare.

"Protection," said Jack.

Ned laughed and gestured at the bleak, treeless landscape around us. "From what? Do you really think it likely that a band of brigands will rise out of the ground and attack us?"

Jack scowled. "You never know."

For once Jack proved to be right about something. No more than ten minutes had passed when I heard a startled cry of "Ho!" from Mr. Armin at the head of the company. I jerked my head in that direction. To my astonishment, a dense patch of furze that lay near the road seemed to be opening up, unfolding like some huge drab and ravaged bud bursting into bloom. From its center emerged not a blossom but a group of five fierce-looking armed men. One of them held a wheel-lock pistol aimed directly at Mr. Armin's chest.

"Dismount!" ordered the bandit, a big-bellied fellow with a filthy, pockmarked face; his bushy black hair and beard were tangled and full of furze twigs. His leaner but equally grimy confederates spread out, swords drawn, to block the road.

Though I was taken aback, I was not as terrified as I would once have been. I had been with the ruthless

Falconer when, unaided, he dispatched or disabled half a dozen brigands with astonishing speed and skill. Mr. Armin had proven himself even more able with a sword than Falconer. I expected that, with the help of the others, he would make short work of these shabby thieves.

Sure enough, instead of swinging from his saddle as he had been commanded to, Mr. Armin spurred his horse forward, at the same time jerking back on the reins so that the animal reared up, front hooves flailing. But the man with the gun, instead of dropping it in panic, calmly took a step backward and fired. The pistol gave off a puff of smoke and a loud report. The black mare gave a sort of shriek and toppled sideways, blood spurting from her neck. Mr. Armin tried to throw himself free, but one foot must have caught in its stirrup, for his leg became pinned underneath his fallen mount.

Despite his bulk, the black-haired man moved swiftly. In an instant he was straddling the fallen rider and had the blade of a dagger pressed against Mr. Armin's throat-bole. "Now the lot of you," he shouted, "dismount and drop your weapons, or watch your friend bathe in his own blood!"

Our hired men's swords clattered onto the stony surface of the road—all except Ned Shakespeare's. "He's bluffing!" Ned whispered to the rest of us.

Jamie Redshaw gave him a look of disgust. With one flick of his walking stick, he knocked Ned's sword from his grasp. Then, wincing at the pain it caused him, he bent and laid the stick carefully on the ground.

"Gather them up!" the leader instructed his companions. When they had done so, he lifted the blade from Mr. Armin's throat and stepped away. "We meant only to relieve you of your money," he told us, "but as you've put me to so much trouble, I believe we'll have the horses as well."

Two of his men took hold of the sharers' mounts. The other two set about unharnessing the teams from the carewares. "Oh, gis!" I murmured. "They'll leave us stranded here!"

Jamie Redshaw nodded grimly. Part of me wanted to urge him to do something, to fight back. But I knew that if he had made a move to do so, I would have tried to hold him back. Now that we had found one another at last, I could not bear to risk losing him.

The leader of the bandits reloaded his pistol, cocked it, and surveyed us prentices and hired men a moment. Then he stepped forward and pressed the muzzle of the gun to Sal Pavy's head. "Which wagon has the money?" he demanded. Sal Pavy was rigid with terror. Tears streamed from his eyes. His chin quivered, but no sound came out.

"It's the rear one," growled Will Sly.

"Thank you," said the brigand, and showed his rotten teeth in a grin. "I didn't want any more trouble. I don't like trouble." He uncocked the pistol, thrust it in his belt, and strode to the back of the nearest careware. But as he reached inside to seize one of the trunks, his hands froze in midair. An unaccountable look of distress came over his pockmarked features. He gave a hoarse cry and took a stumbling step backward, as though his knees had suddenly gone weak.

I was momentarily bewildered by his unexpected reaction. Then Sam's head emerged from within the wagon, and I saw what had alarmed the bandit so. Sam's face had a bluish tinge and was blotched with what looked like open sores. There were dark circles about his reddened eyes; froth flecked the corners of his mouth.

"Water!" he pleaded in a desperate, rasping voice. "Please! I'm dying of thirst!" He reached one shaking hand toward the bandit, and I could see that the skin of it was spotted, too, with red marks surrounded by blue-black patches.

"Saints save us!" I breathed. " 'A's taken wi' the plague!"

18

*D*on't touch me!" cried the black-haired man. In his haste to distance himself from Sam, he collided with the cart wheel. The pistol fell from his belt, but he seemed not to notice. "Come away!" he shouted to his men. "Take nothing with you!" When they hesitated, he bellowed, "Now, you gawking gypes! It's the contagion!"

Sam had climbed out of the careware now, and was staggering about, begging for a drink of water. When he shuffled toward the bandits who were unhitching our horses, they bolted. The other two let go of the sharers' mounts and took to their heels as well.

Now that I could move without fear of being shot or stabbed, I hastened to draw a cup of water from the keg strapped to the side of the careware and held it out to Sam.

"Don't give him that cup!" protested Ned Shakespeare. "He'll contaminate it!"

"Then we'll get another," I said. "Go on, Sam; take it."

Sam turned his hollow eyes gratefully upon me and reached out for the cup. As his trembling hands closed over mine, I gave an involuntary shudder, wondering how much contact was required to transmit the plague from one person to another.

Instead of gulping down the contents of the cup, Sam upended it over his head. The water drenched his tousled, matted hair and coursed down his cheeks. The blotches and sores began to melt away and slough off, as though he had anointed them with water from the Grail. I blinked in astonishment. "What in heaven's name—?" And then the truth struck me like a fool's bladder, and I began to laugh. Sam gave a weak grin and abruptly collapsed in a heap on the ground.

"Help me get him back in the careware," I said to Jamie Redshaw.

He stepped forward uncertainly. "But is he not—"

"Nay, nay," I assured him, still laughing. "It's not the contagion. It's only face paint."

As we lifted him into the wagon, Sam came to and murmured, "I gave a good performance, didn't I?"

"You played the plague to the life," I replied. "Or should I say, to the death." I wet a rag and gently washed the rest of the makeup from his face. "How did you ha' time to do all this?"

He gave me a shamefaced smile. "The truth is, I started on it well before the bandits turned up. I had planned only to play a prank on you and the others."

"It would ha' been a cruel prank," I said. "We were all anxious about you."

"I just meant to give you all a good laugh and liven things up a bit. I'm sorry."

"Well, considering how things turned out, I expect everyone will forgive you." I put a hand on his forehead. "The fever seems to ha' broken. How do you feel?"

"As though my limbs were made of new cheese," he said.

"Rest, then. You'll feel stronger i' the morning."

The rest of the company had managed to lift the dead horse enough to pull Mr. Armin free. He was limping about, rubbing his bruised leg. "You're fortunate it's not broken," said Mr. Phillips.

Mr. Armin did not reply. Though it was too dark to see much, he was staring out across the moor in the direction the brigands had gone. "We should have pursued them," he said grimly, and put a hand to his throat as if feeling again the edge of the bandit's blade.

"How did they hide themselves so well?" asked Jack.

Jamie Redshaw, who was examining the clump of furze from which the thieves had emerged, flipped over one of the shrubs with his walking stick. "They cut some of the furze and covered themselves over with it. A clever tactic."

"Men disguised by bushes," mused Mr. Shakespeare. "I'll have to use it in a play."

"We m-may as well c-camp here for the night," said Mr. Heminges. "I d-doubt those brigands will b-be back."

We pulled the wagons off the road and then used one of

the teams to drag Mr. Armin's mare out of our sight. To my surprise, Mr. Shakespeare got out his travel desk and set it up next to one of the carewares. "You mean to work on the play?" I said. "Out here?"

"Ideas come to me as I ride along," he told me. "If I don't capture them soon, they'll be gone, like those bandits." He lit a horn lantern. "How is Sam?"

"On the mend, I think."

Mr. Shakespeare shook his head. "One hardly knows whether to fine the boy for playing such a stunt or reward him for saving our lives."

"Well, 'a did tell me 'a was sorry. Besides, as they say here in Yorkshire, all's well that ends well."

Mr. Shakespeare smiled and played thoughtfully with the ring in his earlobe. "That's what they say, is it?"

"Aye."

"It's a good line," he said. "Let's give it to Helena."

When we reached Leeds the next day, we were relieved to discover that neither the plague nor the mock players had been there before us. We were even more relieved to find a letter from Sander awaiting us. It did my heart good to hear his voice, which, even on paper, was good-natured and cheerful as a cricket. The letter was a long one, filled with anecdotes about what mischief the boys had been up to and with the latest news about events in London. He mentioned the plague only briefly, near the end of the missive.

Though the death rate is rising, it has not yet reached the proportions everyone feared. Rest assured that all of us here are in good health, aside from a touch of melancholy when we think of you, our absent friends. Mr. Burbage is providing well for us, but asks that you send a share of the box as soon as you are able. For my part, I value your letters more than any amount of money. Good fortune follow you or, even better, precede you.

Yrs. faithfully,

Alexander Cooke

I berated myself for not having written more often, and resolved to get a letter off to him that very evening if I could. Sander would, I knew, be nearly as pleased about my finding a father as I was myself.

My only cause for disappointment was that there seemed to be so little opportunity for Jamie Redshaw and me to discuss the dozens of questions, large and small, that still waited impatiently in the back of my mind, like some important role I had studied but had never been given the chance to perform.

More than anything else I wanted to know about my mother, but even in our rare moments of leisure I could not manage to pry more than a few sentences from him concerning her. It seemed painful for him, as though I were probing at his old war wound and not his memory. I concluded that he must have loved her a great deal, to be hurt so by the thought of her.

We spent a profitable three days in Leeds. Sam had recovered enough to play small parts, provided he rested between scenes. So he would not feel useless, I gave him the book to hold while I took care of the more strenuous stuff. Jamie Redshaw volunteered to take on the task of gatherer. Though the money box must have weighed heavily on his injured back, he bore it without complaint. He went beyond the bounds of duty, in fact, calling enthusiastically to passersby, "Come in and watch the show! Only a penny to see the best that London has to offer!"

One might have thought that Sal Pavy would pitch in and do his part, but, as always, he seemed to consider anything other than acting to be beneath him. In fact, several times he went so far as to chastise me when a property was out of place, as though I were there only to assist him. It was all I could do to keep from assisting him onto the stage with the end of my blunted sword.

I tried hard to be tolerant of him, partly because I wanted to keep peace within the company, and partly because I felt guilty yet about having spied on him. Each time I recalled that path of stripes down his back, I felt a pang of pity that I would not, I am sure, otherwise have had.

To make *King John* more concise and swift-moving, Mr. Shakespeare had pruned most of the female roles, so Sal Pavy and I were conscripted as soldiers for the battle scenes. I spent every spare moment, of which there were few, working on my scriming skills, determined that, if I could not impress Jamie Redshaw with my ability to say lines convincingly, I would at least make a good showing with a sword—something a former soldier could surely appreciate.

Sal Pavy apparently did not consider swordplay a part of acting; for all the pains he took to perfect his delivery of speeches and gestures, I never once saw him practice with a sword or a singlestick. Sam explained this in a hilarious parody of Sal Pavy's well-rounded tones: "It's becauwse at Blackfriahrs, you see, we were not expected to engaige in such uncouth displaiys of aggression."

Whatever instruction he had in scriming must have been minimal, for Sal Pavy's *stoccatas* and edgeblows were clumsy and tentative, not to mention badly aimed. Nor did he content himself with the moves we had rehearsed. When we were on the stage in the second act, locked in mock-mortal combat, he delivered an unexpected down-right blow that caught me unawares and struck my shoulder. It made both of us look foolish—me for dropping my sword, he for standing there looking like a ninny instead of skewering me, as any self-respecting soldier would have done.

The moment we made our exit I turned on him, hot with anger. "Who taught you to sword-fight? Your maiden aunt? You nearly broke me collarbone out there, and I don't think you're up to playing me part as well as your own!"

"Oh, I don't know," he said coolly. "It might be a considerable improvement." To my surprise, he stepped up close to me and peered at my face. "Do you know," he said, "I think you're starting to sprout a few whiskers." Despite myself, I put my hand self-consciously to my chin. Sal Pavy clucked his tongue in mock sympathy. "I wouldn't be surprised if your voice starts to go next."

Though my reason told me not to rise to his taunts, my anger spoke to me in a louder voice. Reaching out, I seized the neck of his leather breastplate and jerked him nearly off his feet. "You'd like it, wouldn't you, an me voice or me collarbone cracked? Because then you'd be able to take over all me best roles, not just a few! I'll wager that blow out there was no accident at all!"

"Boys?" said Mr. Armin as he came off the stage. "Is something amiss?"

Sal Pavy opened his mouth to answer, but I was quicker. "Nay, nay!" I assured him. I let go of Sal Pavy and thumped the front of his breastplate. "Just adjusting his armor. It was chafing him."

Mr. Armin nodded knowingly. "I see. You've taken care of it, then?"

"Oh, aye."

"Good. We wouldn't want any chafing. Would we, Mr. Pavy?"

"No, sir," said Sal Pavy, unable, for once, to quite get his cheerful-and-charming mask properly in place. When I was called upon to deal him a death blow in the next scene, I did it with more conviction than usual—in fact, with great relish. When I was alone behind the stage, I furtively examined myself in the mirror. To my dismay, I found that Sal Pavy was right. A few spindly hairs had made an appearance on my face. I plucked them out ruthlessly with a pair of tweezers.

Unlike most town halls, the one in Leeds had a separate room at one end that we put to use as our tiring-room. As we were changing out of our costumes, Mr. Armin noticed my mother's crucifix, which I had hung around my neck, and inspected it more closely. "That's a fine piece of work," he said. "This is the cross that Redshaw says he gave to your mother?"

Something about the way he put it seemed to suggest that what Jamie Redshaw said was not necessarily what had happened. "Aye," I said defensively. " 'A engraved her name on the back."

Mr. Armin turned over the crucifix. "Yes, I see. A bit of advice. I wouldn't wear that where it may be seen."

"Why not?"

"Folk may take you for a Papist."

"A what?"

"A Catholic. Now, you may be one for all I know, or for all I care. But it's not wise to advertise the fact. There may be no problem here in the north, where Catholics are said to be as common as cowpies, if not quite as visible. But the nearer we get to London, the more chance you'll run afoul of Papist-hating Protestants and bring trouble not only upon yourself but upon the company. We players are held in low enough regard already."

I held up the cross and gazed at it. "Perhaps I should not wear it at all, then."

"That's up to you. If you like, we can put it in the treasury trunk. It'll be safe there."

"All right. I worry about the chain breaking anyway," I said. "Sal Pavy nearly clove it in two out there."

He stepped closer and pulled aside the neck of my linen shirt. "And your collarbone as well, if I'm not mistaken. You'll want to put something on that welt."

"I will."

"If there's trouble between you two," he said, "I'd like to know about it."

"Nay, no trouble."

Smiling skeptically, Mr. Armin said, "I applaud your loyalty, Widge. But don't imagine that we sharers are fooled. We know well enough that Sal Pavy is not the model prentice he pretends to be. He shows a great deal of promise, though, as a player. All he needs is a bit more self-discipline."

I rubbed my shoulder. "And some serious scriming lessons."

Mr. Armin laughed. "I'll work on that. You work on being more tolerant. Bear with him, Widge. He's had a hard time of it."

"Not to hear him talk. 'A makes it sound as though at Blackfriars 'a was treated more like a prince than a prentice—a bedroom of his own, a private tiring-room, no chores of any sort—"

Mr. Armin shook his head soberly. "As I'm sure you realize, he's exaggerating . . . considerably. Come; let's head back, and I'll tell you something of his story." As we walked to the inn, he continued. "I learned what I know from Mr. Pearce, the choirmaster at St. Paul's. Sal was sent there at the age of eight, to be educated and to be trained for the choir. Mr. Pearce tells me he had an extraordinary voice, clear and pure as rain."

"That doesn't sound like such a terrible fate to me."

"It wasn't, of course. But when he was ten or eleven, Sal was forced into service by the Chapel company."

"How could they do that?"

"They kidnapped him, essentially. It's done all the time, and no one dares object, since the Children of the Chapel come under the Queen's direct protection. Theoretically the Chapel company is permitted to take boys only for its choir, but of course their choir doesn't turn a profit, and their acting company does, so you may guess where most of the boys end up—including Sal."

"Why did 'a not simply run off?"

"He did, I gather, several times—and was caught and punished."

I winced. Now I knew the source of those stripes that decorated his back.

"What's more, the masters of the Chapel company all but ruined his singing voice by constantly making him strain to speak his lines *vociferato* and to mimic an old man's voice. Apparently they know no more about vocal techniques than they do about sword techniques. The one good thing to come of all this is that, rather than giving up, Sal determined to be the best actor he could, to draw enough attention to himself to tempt some other company to take him on. And he's done that. We're trying to undo some of the damage that's been done, to his voice and to his . . . to his soul, if you will. If you and Sam can manage to treat him . . . sympathetically, it will help."

I sighed. "I've been trying. It's not easy."

"Nor is what he has been through. His saving grace, and the thing that makes him so gifted an actor, is that he's been able to make use of all those hardships and disappointments. He puts something of himself—his pain, his anger, his frustration, his desires—into every role he plays."

I nodded glumly. "And I do not."

As Sander so often had done, Mr. Armin put a hand on my shoulder, being careful to choose the uninjured one. "You will, Widge, in time. Perhaps you won't be able to truly put yourself into a part until you're a bit more certain who you are."

I had no immediate opportunity to practice being sympathetic to Sal Pavy for, as usual, he did not share our tiring-room, and he made short work of his supper. More unexpected was the absence at supper of two others of our company, Ned Shakespeare and Jamie Redshaw. I tried not to let myself worry over this. Most likely my father was having a drink in some tavern, that was all. But I could not dismiss the nagging notion that he might suddenly have decided he did not particularly want to have a son or to travel with a band of gypsy players, and had gone back to York and his old way of life. He was, after all, as unused to having a son as I was to having a father.

As casually as I could manage, I asked the others if they had noticed him about after the performance. Will Sly recalled seeing him and Ned outside the Golden Lion. There, you see, I told myself, it's just as you imagined; he's only tossing back a few, and will be along in due time.

But night came, and Jamie Redshaw did not. Mr. Shakespeare and I toiled on the third act of *Love's Labour's Won*, but I found it difficult to concentrate, and several times I had to ask Mr. Shakespeare to repeat himself, which galled him, for he was having difficulties of his own. This play was, he swore, the sorriest piece of work he had ever put his hand—or anyone else's—to, and had he not already promised it to the Queen, he'd have gleefully burned it, page by page, like the rubbish that it was.

"Nay," I said, trying to be helpful. "It's not so bad. I've seen any number of plays that were worse: *Fortune's Tennis*, for example, or *The Battle of Alcazar*."

Mr. Shakespeare stared at me as though I'd brought up some subject not fit for polite company. "If I thought for a moment that my work had sunk to the level of those . . . *abominations,*" he said acidly, "I would use my pen knife to open a vein and write a farewell note to the world in my own blood."

"Oh," I said. "I see. The world would not be able to read it, though, you ken, for you'd ha' to write it left-handed."

His look of exasperation gave way slowly, reluctantly, to a sort of smile. "Yes, well, when I reach that point," he said, "I'll be sure to call you in and have you write it for me."

When I returned to our common room, neither Ned nor Jamie Redshaw was there. Though it was late and I was weary, I left the inn and walked through the dark streets of Leeds to the Golden Lion. When I stepped inside the door I saw Jamie Redshaw at once. He and Ned sat at a table with two other men, playing at cards. A haze of pipe smoke hung in the air about their heads. In the center of the table was a pile of coins; smaller piles lay directly before each of the players—except for Jamie Redshaw, who seemed to have not so much as a gray groat.

I nearly turned and left the tavern. I was well aware that the sharers did not approve of gambling; in fact, there were pointed rules against it. Discovering Ned and Jamie Redshaw engaged in this forbidden pastime put me in an awkward position. Clearly it was my duty to report their transgression to the sharers. But if I did, the two would likely be slapped with a substantial fine, and I did not care to be the one responsible. I thought it even possible they might be dismissed—or at least Jamie Redshaw might be;

Mr. Shakespeare would likely be more lenient with his own brother.

As I stood there in the shadows near the doorway, debating with myself, one of the men playing at cards let out a startling whoop of triumph and, leaning across the table, gathered in the central pile of coins. Jamie Redshaw sat even more stiffly than usual, with an equally stiff smile upon his face. "Well," he said with a careless tone that was quite convincing, "easily gotten, easily gone, eh?" He rose carefully to his feet with the aid of his walking stick. "Shall we meet again tomorrow night, gentlemen?"

One of the strangers gave a crooked-toothed grin. "You mean we've not got to the bottom of your purse yet?"

Jamie Redshaw shrugged. "This one, perhaps, but I've several others. Coming, Ned?"

Ned glared grimly down at the pitiful few pennies before him. "Not as long as I've a farthing left."

That should have been my cue to exit, but I missed it. As Jamie Redshaw strode to the door, I shrank back farther in the shadows, not wishing him to know that I had been spying on him. My movement caught his eye, though, and he stopped and raised his cane. "Who's there?" He peered into the dim corner. "Widge?"

"Aye." I came hesitantly forward. "You weren't i' the sleeping room, so I came looking for you."

"Still afraid I'll run off?" He put an arm around my shoulder, making me flinch. "What's wrong?"

"I hurt meself i' the sword fight this afternoon. It's not much; only a bruise." When I thought of his awful war wound, I felt foolish for even mentioning my inconsequential injury. As we headed back to the inn, I said, "Did you watch the play this afternoon?"

"Some of it."

I waited for him to go on, perhaps even to praise me a bit for my performance. When he did not, I prompted him shamelessly. "Did our swordplay look at all real?" I winced again, recalling just how real it had been.

He laughed. "I didn't suppose it was meant to. It was a play."

I nodded glumly. "I suppose it didn't much resemble a real battle."

"No." Abruptly he changed the subject. "You should have joined us at cards."

I wanted to mention the rule against gambling, but I did not wish to seem prudish or chiding, so I said, "I ken naught about card games, and I've no money to wager."

"There were no vast sums involved, just a few pennies to keep the game interesting."

"What that man won looked like more than a few pennies."

"Well, a few shillings, then."

I couldn't help wondering where he'd come by his share of it. "Do you truly ha' several other purses full of money?" I asked.

He laughed. "Of course not. But I couldn't let them think they'd cleaned me out. A fellow has his pride."

I spent a restless night; my mind was still wrestling with the problem of where my loyalties lay. Jack's snoring did not help matters. To get some respite from it, I dragged my sleeping mat out onto the gallery of the inn. As I lay looking up at the stars, I heard a faint sound floating across the inn yard. At first I could not identify it. It blended with the chirping of the crickets and the croaking of frogs, and might have been mistaken for either of them but that it was more sustained and more musical.

Curious, I sat up and listened more closely. Still I could not be certain of its source. When I felt my way down the gallery stairs to the yard, I determined that the sound was coming from the stable. As I drew nearer, it became clear that what I was hearing was a high human voice, a slightly hoarse voice that sometimes wavered, sometimes cracked, but for all that had a haunting, moving quality to it.

It was Sal Pavy, singing.

Immediately after breakfast the next morning Mr. Armin
gathered us prentices in the yard of the inn for a scriming
session. Though the instruction was mainly for Sal Pavy's
benefit, Mr. Armin did not say so, and did not spare Sam
and me in the slightest.

While he worked with Sal Pavy on delivering and parrying edgeblows, Sam and I practiced thrusting, alternating
rapidly between the *imbrocata*, which is delivered above
the opponent's blade, and the *stoccata*, delivered beneath
the opponent's blade. Though our rapiers were blunted,
they were capable of inflicting a nasty bruise, so for protection we strapped on the light, boiled leather breastplates
that passed for metal armor on the stage.

"Why do you smile, infidel," said Sam, "when you are
about to die?"

"I was just recalling the time Nick stuck me wi' his

sword and we all thought 'a'd done me in—all except Sander. There I was, swooning and breathing what I thought were me last breaths, and Sander takes one look and says, 'You sot! He stuck your blood bag!' I didn't feel half a ninny."

Sam grinned and shook his head. "I wish Sander was here now," he said.

I merely nodded. As we were hotly engaged in mock battle, I heard a voice from the second floor gallery say, "It's fortunate that you're playing to townfolk and not to a company of infantrymen." I glanced up to see Jamie Redshaw leaning on the railing, watching our practice.

Mr. Armin and Sal Pavy left off swiping at one another. "Oh," said Mr. Armin coolly. "Why is that?"

Jamie Redshaw laughed a bit uncomfortably, like someone who's been put on the spot. "Well, because they'd hoot you off the stage." He descended the gallery stairs and crossed the cobbles toward us. "I mean, anyone who's ever fought in earnest knows it's nothing like what you're doing." He seemed to realize how condescending this sounded, for he added, "I don't mean to be critical; of course you can't be expected to recreate the feel of a real battle upon the stage."

"No, no," replied Mr. Armin in a tone that might have sounded cordial to someone who did not know him well. "We want to be as convincing as possible. Perhaps you'll give us a few pointers."

Jamie Redshaw shrugged. "If you like."

"Sal, give your sword to Mr. Redshaw, will you?" Sal

Pavy obliged and backed well out of the way. "Now," said Mr. Armin, raising his blade and his eyebrows, "what is it we should be doing, exactly?"

I had the distinct feeling that Mr. Armin was not so much interested in what Jamie Redshaw might teach us as in teaching a lesson of his own, something to do with not putting in one's seven eggs where they're not wanted. I only hoped he would not drive the point home too hard.

Jamie Redshaw seemed to suspect nothing amiss. He came on guard, not in the usual sidewise fencing posture but with his body facing Mr. Armin almost straight on. "First of all," he said confidently, "a fighting man does not waste much time in trading blows. That serves only to tire you out. The object is to put an opponent out of the way with as little ado as possible."

Before he had finished speaking the last word, his blade darted forward, like a striking snake. To my astonishment, Mr. Armin's weapon flew from his grasp and clattered onto the cobbles. Though Mr. Armin was surely as stunned as I, he managed not to show it. His eyes narrowed a little, and he flexed his hand a few times as though it pained him.

It took me a moment to realize what had happened. Jamie Redshaw, instead of engaging his opponent in the usual game of thrust and parry, had disregarded the rules and aimed his point directly at Mr. Armin's sword hand. "The secret, you see," said Jamie Redshaw, "is to do the unexpected."

"Ah," said Mr. Armin, his voice carefully controlled. "Thank you for that insight. Next time I'll know not to expect what I expected. Good day." Jamie Redshaw returned the sword to Sal Pavy and silently left the yard. Mr. Armin turned to us. "Remember that, gentlemen. If you wish to kill your opponent, do the unexpected. If you wish him to live until the next performance, stick to the script. Now, I imagine you're expecting me to assign you fifty *passatas*." He paused. "Well, I'm afraid I'm just hopelessly predictable. Proceed."

As we lined up against the stable wall and began thrusting, Sam said, "Your da made Mr. Armin look a bit of a fool, didn't he?"

I made no reply. I could not make up my mind whether to be proud of Jamie Redshaw's actions, or ashamed.

Mr. Armin had finally finished his play, *Fool Upon Fool*, and our first performance of it did a brisk business. So did our presentation of *King John* in the afternoon. When Jamie Redshaw brought the box to the sharers, his shoulders were sagging under the weight of it. The company's treasury trunk had grown so weighty that it took two men to carry it to the town hall and back. We could not, of course, risk leaving it unattended in our rooms, nor could we spare a man to stay behind and guard it. I was glad to have it close at hand, for it contained not only my future wages but, more important, my mother's crucifix.

At supper that evening, to celebrate our good fortune, the sharers broke out a bottle of brandy from the small stock we carried with us and poured some for everyone—everyone, that is, save Ned Shakespeare and Jamie Redshaw, who were again conspicuously absent. I checked the common sleeping room, but without any real hope that they would be there. They were not. As I started for the stairs, Sam came pounding up them and dragged me back into the sleeping room.

"What's the matter?" I demanded.

"I just overheard Sal Pavy telling Mr. Armin that he saw your father filching money from the box! He says he arrived late for this afternoon's performance, after the entrance doors were opened, and he noticed your da dropping pennies in his purse instead of in the gathering box."

"The devil take him!" I cried. " 'A's lying! Why would 'a lie?"

Sam shrugged. "To make trouble for you?"

"Trouble for me? But why? I've done naught to him!"

"You play the parts he'd like to play," said Sam.

I was speechless with surprise for a moment. Then an alarming thought struck me. "Will they confront me father wi' this, do you think?"

"No doubt."

There was no doubt, either, about where they'd find him and what he'd be doing. "Oh, gis!" I grasped Sam's arm. "You're a good friend, to tell me this. Can you do one more thing? Can you keep them here a minute or two longer?"

"I can try." Sam dashed back downstairs. I exited the room by the gallery door, scrambled down the outer stairs, and ran all the way to the Golden Lion. When I burst through the tavern door, Jamie Redshaw and Ned were at the same table as before, this time with four other men.

As I strode up to them, one of the men rose, scooped up his small stock of money, and made a quick departure. Thanks to the haze of tobacco smoke, which made the dim interior of the tavern even dimmer, I did not get much of a look at the man, but his portly build and the eye patch he wore were familiar.

"Why are you dropping out so sudden?" called one of the other cardplayers, but the one-eyed fellow did not bother to reply, or even to look back.

I stopped at Jamie Redshaw's side and bent to whisper in his ear, "I think the sharers may be on their way here."

"Yes?" he said without looking up from his cards.

"You don't want them to find you gambling!" I said urgently.

"Why not?"

"There's a company rule against it!"

"Ah." He stood at once and gathered up the sizable pile of coins that lay before him. "Gentlemen, I must ask you to excuse me as well. Ned, I think you'll also want to depart."

"What?" protested one of their playing companions. "You've got to give us a chance to win some of our money back!"

"Another time, gentlemen, another time. Let's go out the back way," he said to me.

With Ned Shakespeare along, I did not feel I should bring up the matter of Sal Pavy's accusation. Instead, I said, "Who was that wight wi' th' eye patch?"

"He didn't mention his name," replied Jamie Redshaw. "Why?"

"I believe 'a's wi' Lord Pembroke's Men. I saw him in their company, back in Newark."

"Did you? Perhaps he's spying on us."

"If so," said Ned, "he learned little, and it cost him dearly. How much did you win from him and the others?"

Jamie Redshaw cupped his purse in one hand, as though weighing it. "A fair amount. How much did you lose?"

"A fair amount," said Ned sourly. He glanced over at me. "You'll say nothing to the others about . . . about what we were up to?"

I shook my head. "Nay. That is," I added, "an you promise to go and sin no more."

Jamie Redshaw laughed. "The boy drives a hard bargain. What do you say, Ned? Shall we forswear gambling?"

"If we must," Ned said grudgingly. "I don't care for all these petty rules of the company's. It's like being back in Stratford, but with four parents riding me rather than just two."

When we reached the inn Ned went inside, but I held Jamie Redshaw back. "I . . . I don't mean to pry, but you told me last night you'd been cleaned out."

"And so I was."

"Then what . . . I mean, where . . ."

"Where did I get the money to wager tonight?"

"Aye."

He raised his walking stick. For a moment I feared he

meant to strike me with it for my impudence and, from old habit, I ducked my head. But he only tossed it lightly into the air and caught it again. "I wagered this. In truth, I've made far more use of it as a gambling stake than as a sword."

I laughed, more with relief than amusement. "I was right, then. 'A was lying."

"Who?"

"Sal Pavy. 'A—'a accused you of taking money from the box."

"The little weasel! He needs a sound thrashing!"

"Nay, nay. Let it pass, please!"

"Let it pass? He's insulted my honor!"

"Aye, but it's not worth stirring up trouble i' the company over 't."

"Not worth it?" Jamie Redshaw shook his head. "If you think that, you have a good deal to learn about the importance of honor."

"No doubt. But I ken a lot already about th' importance of keeping peace wi'in the company."

"Then you need to teach it to your friend Master Pavy."

" 'A's no friend of mine. But I don't wish him to be an enemy, either."

"There is no middle ground. If you can't count a man your friend, then you must count him your enemy."

I stared at him, trying to read his face in the dark. "You truly believe that?"

"I've had to," he said, "in order to survive."

"In battle, you mean. But not in ordinary life, surely?"

He let the walking stick drop to his side, and its metal tip clanged on the cobbles. "All of life is a battle."

When we entered the main room of the inn, Mr. Armin still sat at our table, with a pint of ale in his hands. He glanced up at me. "Mr. Shakespeare's waiting for you," he said. "Mr. Redshaw, I'd like a word with you."

As I headed for the stairs, I caught Jamie Redshaw's eye and gave him a pleading glance that said, "Please don't make trouble for me."

Though I was distracted with wondering what went on downstairs, I managed to do a fair job of transcribing. We were into the fourth act of what Mr. Shakespeare was now calling *All's Well That Ends Well*. I was delighted to have made such a significant contribution to the play, but he was as unhappy as ever. In the past week or so, he had taken to muttering to himself, like a litany, "Something's missing; something's missing." But he seemed unable to hit upon just what the missing thing was.

I was anxious to cheer him up, but I knew that I must be cautious in what I said, lest I make his melancholy mood worse. "Perhaps you're being too harsh in your judgment of the play," I ventured. "It seems to me to ha' quite a number of good things in 't."

I half expected him to reply, as he had before, "What do

you know about it?" He did look peevish but instead of berating me he challenged me: "Name one."

"Well . . . there's Helena."

He rolled his earring about between thumb and finger
meditatively. "You like her, do you?"

"Oh, aye. In truth, I admire her. She's loyal, she's clever,
she's strong-willed. She kens exactly what she wants, and
she'll not be deterred."

"Yes, yes, I grant you that. But however strong she may
be, she cannot carry a play all by herself."

"Why not?"

He sighed. "I don't have the time just now to give you a
course in how to construct a well-made play."

"I'm sorry. I was only trying to understand."

"I know, I know." He toyed with his earring again for a
time and then went on. "A play is like a balance, you
see. If, on one end of the arm, you place a certain quantity
of loyalty and cleverness and strong will, on the other
end you need an equal weight of something else, to off-
set it."

"Well, you ha' Bertram. 'A's selfish and haughty and
rude." Though I did not say so, I was thinking what a pity
it was that Sal Pavy had not yet graduated to men's roles,
for he could have played Bertram to the life without any effort at all.

"But Bertram is no villain—nor can we let him be, or the
audience will never accept the notion that Helena is in
love with him so unswervingly."

"An you love someone," I said, "do you not overlook their faults?"

"Only to a point. No, we can't depend on Bertram to bring things into balance. Let's leave him in the middle, halfway between Helena on the one hand and, on the other hand, someone . . . someone truly despicable. But *what* someone?" He pressed a hand to his head and sighed again. "Never attempt to write a play, Widge," he said.

"I had no plans to."

"Good. They always betray you. When you're only imagining them, they seem so ideal, so full of promise and possibility. Then, when you try to get them down on paper, they turn on you and refuse to live up to your expectations."

One of the uncanny qualities about Mr. Shakespeare's words, I had learned, was that, however general they might seem, at the same time they somehow managed to speak directly to each individual who heard them, and to address his particular plight. "Perhaps the fault is ours," I said, "in hoping for too much. We cannot expect people to be flawless."

"People?" he said. "I thought we were speaking of plays."

I smiled sheepishly. "Of course. I was only—"

"I know." Wearily he closed his eyes and rubbed at his forehead. Then abruptly he stopped and raised his head, his eyes wide open. "I know," he repeatedly softly. "I know. I know who he is."

"Who *who* is?"

"The someone. The balancing someone. The despicable someone." As I had seen it do before, Mr. Shakespeare's mood transformed in the space of a few seconds from melancholy to manic. "He's a soldier—a friend of Bertram's, but not a true friend. He's a braggart. He's deceitful. He's a coward. Bertram, though, will not hear a word against him—like Helena, he's loyal—" Mr. Shakespeare waved his good hand at me. "Go back, go back," he commanded.

"Back?" I echoed.

"To Act One. We'll write him in."

I flipped frantically through the pages of the script. "What's his name to be, then?"

"I don't know. Something despicable. *Menteur. Poltron.* It doesn't matter. Just write."

And we were off, galloping once again. The demands of keeping up with the stampede of words that followed put all thought of Jamie Redshaw and Sal Pavy's accusation out of my mind for the moment. When Mr. Shakespeare was done with me at last and I hurried back down to the main room, I found Mr. Armin and Jamie Redshaw still there, and not at one another's throats but conversing amiably over their ale. "How did it go?" asked Mr. Armin—the very words I would have liked to ask.

"Quite well," I said. " 'A was a bit downcast at first, but that's naught of note."

Mr. Armin nodded. "He can hardly expect to write *Hamlet* every time. By the bye, he's told me he greatly appreciates your help and your patience."

"Has 'a, truly?" I said. " 'A seldom says so to me face."

"It's not his way." Mr. Armin turned to Jamie Redshaw. "Widge has been a valuable addition to our company, sir."

If I hoped to see some trace of fatherly pride, I was disappointed. Jamie Redshaw simply said, "I'm glad to hear it," then got stiffly to his feet. "I believe I'll retire." He waved a stack of handbills at me. "I've been given the job of posting these around town in the morning."

I would have left with him, for I hoped to learn what had been said in regard to Sal Pavy's charge. But Mr. Armin asked me to stay. It took him several minutes to get to what was on his mind. Finally he said, "How much do you know of this Redshaw?"

"Well . . . very little, I suppose," I admitted reluctantly. "I ken 'a's me father."

"Has he said so?"

"Not in as many words. But 'a was . . . well acquainted wi' me mother. They would ha' wed, 'a said, had it not been for her parents' objections."

"You're certain he knew her?"

" 'A kenned her name, and that it was engraved on the crucifix. Why? Do you doubt him?"

"I've no real reason to, just . . . just a feeling."

"What sort of feeling?"

"That not everything he says is so. For example, his statement that he and your mother were well acquainted implies that he grew up here in Yorkshire. Yet his speech says otherwise. I put him down as a Dorset man, or Somerset."

" 'A never said 'a grew up here. Besides, 'a's spent many years in other lands, as a soldier."

"So he says."

"You doubt that, too?" I tried to keep my tone calm and reasonable but did not entirely succeed.

Mr. Armin shrugged. "As I said, I've no real reason to, so let's let it drop for now. I can see it's upsetting you, and I can't blame you."

I was upset mainly because Mr. Armin was bringing into the light a shadowy something that I myself had secretly suspected but had always managed to dismiss. After all, I told myself, who was I to condemn a man for the occasional falsehood? Besides, even if Jamie Redshaw did stray from the truth from time to time, it did not mean that he had lied about everything. In any case, I felt it was my duty to defend him. "I suppose you have him down as a thief, too, on Sal Pavy's say-so?"

"No. Clearly not everything that Sal says can be counted on, either."

"Oh." My anger subsided a bit at this. "You did not accuse him, then?"

"I told him that Sal had accused him."

"And what did 'a do?"

"He laughed. And then he admitted that he had indeed taken several coins from the box."

My heart sank at his news. " 'A did?"

Mr. Armin nodded, then fished in his wallet and held out something for me to see. "They were these." In his hand were three circles the exact size of a penny but made of

wood, with some silvery substance—quicksilver, perhaps—
rubbed on the surface.

"Wooden coins?" I said.

"Coney-coins, some call them."

I shook my head in disgust. "What sort of wight would
do such a thing?"

"A woodman?" suggested Mr. Armin slyly.

"Aye," I said, "a woodman would. Particularly a woodman who's wood," I added, certain that Mr. Armin would
know that, hereabouts, *wood* was used to mean "insane."

He smiled appreciatively. "Aye, a wood woodman would,
though I would 'a would not."

I could provide no further puns, only a prodigious yawn.
In the street outside the inn a night watchman cried, "Ten
o'clock, and all's well!"

"Holy mother," I said wearily. "I hope so."

When we headed for the town hall next afternoon, I noticed that many of the town's walls and fences still sported
handbills for yesterday's *King John*, and only a very few
held papers announcing that day's performance of *The Two
Gentlemen of Verona*. In addition, most of the *Two Gentlemen* handbills had no date or time printed on them. "Oh,
gis," I said to Sam. " 'A's not done his job!"

"Your da?" Sam said.

I nodded grimly. Even worse, when half past one came
around, Jamie Redshaw did not turn up to act as gatherer.
"I'll do it," Sam offered.

"Nay," I said, "you're still not strong. You help wi' makeup. I'll gather."

Sal Pavy arrived late, as was his habit lately. When he saw me holding the box, he smirked and shook a finger at me as if to say, "No filching, now." The gesture I gave him in return could not have been so readily translated, at least not by a person of good upbringing.

Jamie Redshaw did show up for supper, for a change. When Mr. Armin asked why he had not done his duty as gatherer, he said, with evident surprise and chagrin, "I assumed that, after yesterday, you would prefer that I not handle the money."

"If I implied that, I did not mean to," said Mr. Armin.

"There's the m-matter of the h-handbills, too," said Mr. Heminges. "You were t-to replace yesterday's with today's."

"I know, and I apologize. The truth is—" He paused, looking uncomfortable. "Well . . . it's difficult, as an old soldier, to admit this but . . . I was ambushed."

"Ambushed?" said Ned Shakespeare with an incredulous laugh.

Jamie Redshaw cast him a look sharp enough to sober him. "Attacked, if you will. I had posted but a few of the bills when I passed the mouth of a narrow alley. A moment later, someone struck me from behind with a cudgel or the like. When I fell to my knees, dazed, my assailant snatched the bills from my hand; before I could recover, he had vanished."

Mr. Armin frowned skeptically. "Why would anyone wish to steal our handbills?"

"You would know that better than I."

"For the same reason they'd set fire to our carts," said Jack resentfully. "To make life difficult for us." It was now Jack's lot to sleep in one of the carewares each night, lest they be molested again. Though it might be uncomfortable for him, it was a blessing for the rest of us, to be spared his snoring.

"Well," said Mr. Heminges, "they c-certainly succeeded. The audience was f-far smaller today; p-presumably folk thought we were d-doing *King John* again."

"It must be a rival company, then," said Mr. Phillips. "But whose?"

"Lord Pembroke's Men?" I suggested.

"We d-don't know that they're in the v-vicinity, Widge."

"But I—I think I saw one of them yesterday." I noticed Ned Shakespeare giving me a warning look, as though reminding me not to divulge under what circumstances I had seen the man. "The wight wi' th' eye patch."

"I don't recall anyone of that description among Pembroke's men," said Mr. Phillips.

"Nor do I," said Mr. Shakespeare. "But they may well have altered the company for touring purposes, as we have done."

"They were at Newark, too," I reminded them. "When the carewares were set afire."

"B-but what do they have to g-gain by harassing us?" said Mr. Heminges.

Will Sly shrugged. "Simple. If they run us off, they'll have that much less competition."

Mr. Armin still looked skeptical. "I find it hard to imagine them stooping to such base tactics, a respectable company like Pembroke's."

"In desperate straits," said Jamie Redshaw, "respectable men sometimes cease to be respectable." He rose from the table. "If you'll excuse me, I mean to go and lie down. My head is still throbbing."

"I'll bring you up some willow bark tea," I said.

He gave me a dubious look. "I'd prefer brandy."

"Nay, nay," I protested. "Spirits will only make your head ache worse."

"I'll vouch for that," said Will Sly, and the others laughed, for Will was known for his tendency to overindulge in drink from time to time.

When I brought the tea to the common room, Jamie Redshaw was not lying down, but standing in the open doorway to the gallery, looking out on the inn yard. He turned to me. "Your Mr. Armin seems suspicious of me, somehow. Has he said anything of the sort to you?"

"Nay," I lied. "I suppose 'a's just naturally a suspicious fellow." As soon as the words left my mouth, I felt guilty, for I well knew that Mr. Armin was a fair man, and that, if he seemed mistrustful or wary at times, it was only because he was concerned about my welfare, or that of the company.

We sat on our traveling trunks, and I poured some of the willow bark tea into an earthenware cup. Jamie Redshaw took a sip of it and made a face. "I still say it would be better with a dollop of brandy—a large one." He set the cup aside. "You seem to have taken on the duties of physician as well as clerk and actor. You should demand an increase in wages."

I shook my head emphatically. "I would never dare do that."

"Why not? You deserve it. You heard how highly Armin spoke of you. Shall I do the asking for you?"

I shook my head again, even more emphatically. "I've no wish to appear greedy. They might conclude they could do wi'out me."

"So? There are other companies. Perhaps one of them would better appreciate your worth."

The mere thought of leaving the Lord Chamberlain's Men sent a stab of dread through me, like the mention of the plague. "Nay! You can't ask me to give up me position here!"

Jamie Redshaw held up a hand to calm me. "I'm not asking that. It was but a suggestion. I've no right to tell you what to do."

"You're—you're me father," I said.

He looked uncomfortable, as though his head or his war wound were bothering him. "Well," he said, "you've done well enough without me up until now."

I gave a bitter laugh. "For the past year or so, aye," I said, more hotly than I intended. "For the fourteen years before that, I was not doing so well for meself. I could have used a father then."

Jamie Redshaw seemed taken aback by my outburst. "I'm sorry," he replied, though not very sympathetically. "As I've said, I had no idea you existed." He scowled and rubbed the back of his head. "I'm feeling a bit dizzy. I need to rest now." He stretched out on his mattress and closed his eyes.

Though he obviously meant for me to depart, I stubbornly lingered. "I was only wondering . . . that is . . . I ken how reluctant you are to speak of me mother, but . . . "

"But you want to know more about her."

"Aye," I said eagerly. "And about yourself as well."

He turned his head to me and opened his eyes. "Why?"

"Why? Well, so that . . . so that I ken something of where I come from, I suppose."

"That's not important," he said. "All that truly matters is where you end up." It was very nearly the same thing Mr. Armin had said to me a few weeks earlier, and it was not what I wanted to hear. "One thing I can tell you," he went on. "You don't want to end up like me." He turned away again. "I'll try to recall more about your mother, and we'll talk again. We've plenty of time."

But the right time seemed never to come. When the players were on the road, Jamie Redshaw and I were continually in the company of the other prentices and hired men, and though I could count Sam and Will Sly my friends, I could not say the same for Jack and Ned and Sal Pavy. Certainly I would not have cared to discuss so personal a matter before them.

When we were in residence in some town, our mornings were occupied with rehearsing and occasional lessons, and our afternoons with performing. In the evenings Jamie Redshaw was seldom at the inn with the rest of us. I suspected that he and Ned were, despite their pledge, still tarrying in the local alehouses, though heaven only knew what they found to wager with.

The sharers' plan—to play only the larger towns and thus avoid being associated with the company of thieves who were passing themselves off as players—proved to be flawed. The most populous places were, we found, also the ones most susceptible to the plague. Some of these contagion-racked cities turned away all travelers; others seemed to have a special dislike of theatre companies. The officials of some towns drove us off with threats; others paid us substantial sums not to perform.

When we reached Shrewsbury, which sat off the main road a little way, we found signs posted outside the town, forbidding anyone at all to enter. "That's unfortunate," said Mr. Heminges. "We're short on s-supplies."

"They can't keep us out," said Jamie Redshaw indignantly and, gripping his walking stick like a cudgel, strode forward, past the sign and up the broad main street. He had not gone fifty yards before the first men began to emerge from taverns and shops. Several had swords drawn. One—a tavern keeper, judging from his apron—carried a gun, a wide-barreled matchlock blunderbuss.

"In case you can't read," he called out, "the sign says no travelers allowed!"

Jamie Redshaw halted. "We need food and drink!"

"Go back beyond the sign, then. We'll bring it to you!"

When Jamie Redshaw rejoined the company, Mr. Armin said, "We would have handled the matter, Mr. Redshaw. It's not your concern."

Jamie Redshaw smiled, more smugly than apologetically, I thought. "My stomach is my concern," he said.

A short while later, a small group of men, led by the tavern keeper with the blunderbuss, approached us. One of the men carried a large basket of viands—cheese, bread, dried fish, apples—and another a small keg of ale. They set the provisions in the road. "That's seven shillings' worth," said the tavern keeper. "Put your coins in the plague stone."

"The p-plague stone?" repeated Mr. Heminges.

The man pointed to a limestone boulder that sat beside the road. A sort of bowl had been carved into the top of it, and this depression was filled with water. Mr. Heminges dropped a half-angel and two shillings into it.

I leaned over to whisper to Sam, "They must imagine that the water somehow drowns the infection."

"Doesn't it?" said Sam.

"I don't ken," I replied and, more irritably, added, "Why does everyone seem to think I'm a physician? I'm an actor."

"I can see that," Sam said calmly. "This is your impersonation of Sal Pavy, right?"

I tried to glare at him, but it somehow turned into a grin. "You sot."

In Telford we found that we had once again been preceded by the band of thieves posing as players. There was a new development in their deceit, now, though; this time they were calling themselves the Lord Chamberlain's Men.

The mayor pointed out to us one of the handbills the counterfeit company had posted, announcing a performance that the mayor paid for but never saw. The play it purported to advertise was none other than Mr. Shakespeare's *King John*.

"Gog's blood!" I said to Jamie Redshaw. "Now we ken who stole the bills from you, and why!"

I expected him to react with anger and vow to catch the culprits. Instead, he shook his head, tapped the handbill with the head of his walking stick, and said with something like admiration, "Well, there's no denying they're cheeky, clever rascals, is there?"

We moved on to Bridgnorth, where we played a single performance of *Fool Upon Fool*, then took ourselves to Kidderminster. Like most of the towns we had played since leaving Leeds, these were not on the itinerary I had sent to Sander. "An we play none of the places we planned to," I complained to Sam, "how can we ever hope for a letter from London to find us?"

Since few of these smaller towns had halls big enough to accommodate us, we often had to set up our wagon-bed stage in the courtyard of the inn where we were lodging. It was far from the ideal playing space; the boards sagged and swayed under our feet and, because the stage was so much smaller than we were used to, we were in constant danger of stepping off the edge.

In fact, I did just that during my *King John* sword-fighting scene with Sal Pavy. I was wary of his wild edgeblows still, and spent a good deal of my time retreating. He failed to warn me that I had run out of room, so off I went and landed, luckily, in the arms of one of the audience. For my pains, I got a round of laughter and applause.

As with the blow he'd delivered to my collarbone, I was

certain this had been no accident. Though I was furious, I neither confronted him nor complained to the sharers. Jamie Redshaw, who had seen me take the fall, urged me to retaliate in kind. "The next time you play the scene, let him have an 'accidental' thrust to the groin. He'll never expect it—and it's certain he'll never forget it."

I laughed weakly. " 'A deserves as much. But I cannot. I've promised Mr. Armin I'd be patient wi' him."

"It was a fool's promise. I know how boys like this Pavy work. If you don't strike back, he'll continue to push and push you until he's pushed you out of the picture." He gave me a searching glance. "You're not afraid of him, are you?"

"Of course not," I replied indignantly.

"Good. Then show him."

There would be no opportunity to exact revenge on Sal Pavy until we played *King John* again, which likely would not be for a week or so. Our next stop was Worcester—a town that was, for a change, actually on our itinerary. I was prepared to perform at an inn once more, but Worcester proved to have an actual theatre, built as a venue for gypsy companies like ours—one reason why our sharers had put it on their schedule. Several other companies, we learned, had been here before us, including a much-reduced Lord Admiral's Men and a scaled-down version of the Earl of Derby's Men.

When we emerged from the town hall, having secured permission to play two afternoon performances, we discovered a bedraggled troupe of players who had, presumably, come there for the same purpose. Every member of the company was afoot. Their single careware, which looked about to collapse, was pulled by two horses in much the same state. Though they wore no special livery, Mr. Armin recognized them as the Earl of Hertford's Men. He greeted the man who headed up the sorry-looking company, a tall, underfed fellow with crooked teeth, who would have looked more at home in a wheat field, chasing crows, than on a stage.

"Hello, Martin! You and your men look as though you're a bit down on your luck."

The man named Martin looked over our company, who were clad in our fine blue caps and capes. "And you look as though you've prospered."

"Only lately. We've had our share of hard times, too."

"I suppose you've gotten permission to play here already." At Mr. Armin's nod, Martin scowled. "We were counting on a brief engagement here to give us enough funds to limp back to London. We've already sold our livery, our best horses, and one of our wagons; we've nothing left to sell save our costumes and the clothes on our backs."

The sharers offered to let them perform in our place, but Hertford's Men refused. "That would be unfair," said Martin.

"Well, suppose we toss a coin," said Mr. Armin.

Martin shook his head. "Too arbitrary. I propose, instead, that we hold an acting competition. The players who acquit themselves best in the opinion of the audience will then get to perform for profit. What say you?"

After a moment's consultation, the sharers accepted the challenge. "Shall we say here, before the town hall, at four o'clock?" said Mr. Armin. "We'll send a crier around town to announce it."

That gave us a scant hour to decide what scene we would enact, with what actors, and to prepare ourselves. "It should b-be a scene with a m-man and a woman," said Mr. Heminges. "Those g-go over best."

"And a comic scene is most likely to win the audience over quickly," added Mr. Phillips.

"What about Viola and Feste's scene from *Twelfth Night*?" suggested Sam.

"Too insubstantial, I think," said Mr. Shakespeare. "We need something with more weight to it."

"Lavinia's scene with the staff, from *Titus*, then," said Mr. Armin.

Will Sly laughed. "Oh, yes, that's comical, that is. A ravaged girl reveals who it was that lopped off her hands and cut out her tongue. It'll have the audience rolling about on the ground."

"It's to be an acting contest," Mr. Armin reminded him, "not a jesting contest."

"Lord Hertford's Men are so d-defeated already," said Mr. Heminges, "p-perhaps we should let them win."

"Deliberately do our worst, you mean?" said Mr. Shakespeare. "No. I'm sure they'd prefer to lose, rather than to win that way."

Lord Hertford's Men did choose a comic scene, one from Peele's *The Old Wives' Tale,* and the audience responded with gales of laughter. By contrast, when Sal Pavy did his wordless turn as the unfortunate Lavinia, there was, as usual, scarcely a sound. But when we were done and those watching were asked to indicate their favorite, the applause given our scene was by far the heartier.

Though I had no right to be jealous, I was—fiercely so. I had been with the company far longer than Sal Pavy, after all, and the role had been mine before it was his. Why should I not be the one up there basking in the applause?

Lord Hertford's Men accepted their lot with good grace, consoled somewhat by the fact that our sharers offered to buy most of their wardrobe for considerably more than it was worth. We had no real need for the costumes, of course, nor any extra room in our carewares; it was a way of aiding a troupe of our fellows who were less fortunate than we, without wounding their pride.

In the morning Will Sly and I and Jamie Redshaw went about Worcester, putting up announcements for that afternoon's performance of *The Two Gentlemen of Verona.*

Since the whole town could be traversed in ten minutes' time, the job did not require three of us; we only wanted to be certain that our handbills did not fall into the hands of some rival company again.

As we toured the town, Jamie Redshaw made a note of where the alehouses were. "Care to join me for a drink after the play?" he asked Will Sly.

"Thanks, but I'd liefer do my drinking at the inn," said Will, "where I'm not so likely to be drawn into a game of chance."

"You have a weakness for gambling, then, do you?" asked Jamie Redshaw.

"I have a weakness for everything. I've learned that my only hope lies in staying in sight of the sharers. They have a way of keeping at bay anything that looks remotely like a vice or pleasure."

"Now, that's unfair," I said, though I could not help laughing a little. "They're only trying to keep the company respectable, and give the lie to th' image of players as disreputable wights."

"It seems to me," said Jamie Redshaw, "that they're trying a trifle too hard."

The sharers were cautious in other ways, too. After Sam's bout of ague, they had begun to insist that each of us learn several of our fellow players' parts, so that if one of the company was injured or fell ill, another could fill the breach. So it was that when Jack, against everyone's advice, ate some suspicious-looking brawn at lunch and came down with a gripe in his guts, Ned Shakespeare was able, if not exactly willing, to fill in for him.

Since Jack would be confined to our room anyway, we left the treasury trunk in his care, with instructions to keep both doors barred until our return. I gave him peppermint oil to settle his stomach, then set out for the theatre.

As I mounted the steps to the stage, I heard Ned's complaining voice say, "I don't see why you can't press Jamie Redshaw into service."

The voice that replied was his brother's. "Because we cannot afford to pay out another hired man's wages."

"Can't afford it?" exclaimed Ned. "The treasury trunk is near to overflowing!"

"And we've rents to pay upon our return, and new costumes to buy, and a hundred other expenses you know nothing of." Though Mr. Shakespeare's tone was reasonable enough, Ned was clearly rankled by it.

"Yes, well, Redshaw's paying himself a good wage, anyway," said Ned spitefully. "You may as well make him work for it." He emerged, scowling, from behind the curtain, gave me a quick and hostile glance, and then pushed past me.

I stepped through the curtain. Mr. Shakespeare sat before a polished metal mirror, trying without the use of his right hand to turn his features into those of Antonio. He glanced up at my reflection. "When did you say this plaster bandage can come off?"

"I didn't say. I'd only be guessing."

He sighed. "Well, if I can put up with it until we reach Stratford, I can consult the family's physician there. I presume he knows something about broken bones."

"I would not be too confident of it. Most physicians, I think, dislike the messier aspects of medicine. They prefer to dispense pills and nostrums."

"You may be right," he said.

I opened the costume trunk and dug out my dress for Silvia. "I . . . I overheard what Ned was saying."

"I'm sorry you did."

"Did 'a mean to say that me father is filching from the box?"

"Most likely." Mr. Shakespeare paused. "I mean that it's most likely what Ned was implying, not that your father is most likely stealing money."

"Oh. Do you think Ned may ha' seen it happen?"

"What I think is that Ned will say whatever suits his purpose at the moment." He flung his makeup brush down in frustration.

"Shall I help you?" I asked.

He shook his head. "I'd like to think I'm not totally helpless." He turned and gazed in the direction Ned had gone. "It was a mistake, bringing him along. He's been more of a hindrance than a help, I think." I made no reply, for I felt he was talking more to himself than to me. "But," he went on, "he is family, and we must make allowances for family."

To this I did reply, for the observation seemed to extend

to me and Jamie Redshaw. "Aye," I said. "They may not be as we'd have them be, so I suppose we must take them as they are, mustn't we?"

Mr. Shakespeare gave a rueful half smile. "Oh, Lord, sir," he said.

The other players arrived, one by one, and set about transforming themselves into their characters. Beyond the curtain, I could hear the audience filling up the hall, getting their coughs out of the way before the play began, talking to one another in curiously hushed tones, like people anticipating some momentous event. As always, it was both heady and at the same time humbling to think that we were that event.

Just before we were ready to go on, a small, nearly bald man poked his head tentatively around the curtain. "I'm the town clerk," he said. "Are you the Lord Chamberlain's Men?"

"Yes," said Mr. Heminges, "and we have p-papers to prove it."

"It's not that I doubted you," said the man, coming all the way around the curtain. "I only wanted to be sure I was putting this into the proper hands." He held out a folded paper sealed with wax. Mr. Heminges took it, read the back, and passed it on to me. "From S-Sander," he said.

My hand trembled with eagerness. "Dare I read it now?" I asked.

"Of c-course," said Mr. Heminges. "The audience c-can wait a few m-minutes more. B-but you must read it aloud."

"Aye." I broke the seal and unfolded the missive. I had expected another long, reassuring letter full of news and amusing anecdotes. It was, instead, succinct—two short paragraphs without even a greeting—and far from reassuring:

This is but one of half a dozen letters sent to various towns along your route, in hopes that one of them will reach you. The situation here is growing grave. The contagion has become more of a threat. None of us has been afflicted so far. Mr. Burbage has departed for the country, though, to escape it.

He left us a substantial sum, of course, but it has dwindled rapidly, for we have been obliged to pay a physician to tend Mr. Pope, who has fallen ill. The doctor calls it a stroke, and is bleeding him regularly. Goody Willingson and I are doing the best we can with the boys and Tetty, but I do not know how much longer our food and our funds will hold out. I know that the company may well be in reduced circumstances, too, but if there is any way you can send us even a pound or two, it would be a great relief.

Your obt. svt.,
Alexander Cooke

When I had finished reading, my fellow players stood in shocked silence a moment. Then Mr. Armin said, "What date did he put on the letter?"

"Twenty-four July."

"And this is the third of August. They must be in desperate straits by now."

"The quickest w-way would be for one of us t-take the money to them," said Mr. Heminges.

"I'll do it," I said at once. "Except for Sam, I'm the smallest and lightest."

Mr. Armin placed a hand on my shoulder. "Thanks for the offer. We really should have a more experienced rider, though—and a more experienced swordsman, I suspect, for there may be bandits along the way."

"I agree," said Mr. Heminges. Mr. Shakespeare and Mr. Phillips nodded.

"I'll depart immediately after the play, then," said Mr. Armin.

I stared at him incredulously. "*After* the play? Why not now?"

"Two hours cannot make much difference."

So distressed was I that I forgot all my resolve never to put my place with the company in peril by complaining or quarreling. "How do you ken that?" I said. "They may be starving even as we speak! Suppose they've run out of money to pay the physician?"

"We're players," said Mr. Armin. "We have a performance to give."

"Is a performance worth more than a life, then?" I cried. "We're merely to act, when we should be taking action?"

"That's enough, W-Widge," said Mr. Heminges.

I turned to him. "If none of you will go, then send me

father." Mr. Heminges shook his head. "Why not?" I demanded.

He seemed about to reply, and then Jamie Redshaw came around the curtain and set the gatherer's box down with a thump. "The audience is growing restless," he announced. He looked around at our solemn and strained expressions. "Is something wrong?"

"We'll explain later," said Mr. Heminges.

"Oh. Very well." Wincing, Jamie Redshaw hefted the box. "I'll take this back to the inn, then, and add it to the treasury trunk."

"G-good. Widge, g-go and get your play book, and we'll begin."

Though there was far more I wished to say about the matter, I feared I had said too much already. I clamped my mouth tight shut and, like a good prentice, did as I was told. I took my place in the wings as prompter until my time came to go on the stage. But tears of frustration stung my eyes so that, when Ned Shakespeare needed to be told his lines, I could not make out the words upon the page.

Though the actors said their speeches with unprecedented speed, the play seemed interminable. The moment Mr. Armin delivered his last line, he strode from the stage, tossed off his costume, and donned his street garb. I should have assisted him, I suppose, but I was too angry with him still.

As I was changing from my costume, it occurred to me that, if I could send a note of some sort with him, it might help cheer Sander and the others. Without even pausing to put away my wig and costume, I dashed from the theatre and down the street. I ran directly to the stable at the inn, supposing I would find Mr. Armin saddling one of the horses.

I supposed wrong. As I emerged into the yard, I saw that the door to our common sleeping room stood open, so I scrambled up the gallery stairs. When I burst through the doorway, I came upon a scene so unexpected that, despite my breathless condition, I gave a startled gasp.

Mr. Armin knelt on the floor next to the limp, sprawled form of Jack, who was clearly unconscious—or dead. My immediate thought was that his illness, which I had taken to be minor, had been worse than I suspected. And then I caught sight of the treasury trunk, which sat close at hand. Its hasp was twisted, its lid nearly torn from its hinges, and there was not a single coin within. Next to it sat the gatherer's box, every bit as empty.

*G*og's wounds!" I gasped. "What's happened?"

It was a foolish thing to say, for it was perfectly clear what had happened. Someone had assaulted Jack and made off with all our money. Mr. Armin did not bother to state the obvious, but said, "He's alive; I can feel a pulse in his neck. Help me lift him onto his bed."

As I hurried to take hold of Jack's legs, I got my first good look at his head as well. It lay in a pool of blood. When we had him laid out upon the mattress, I said, "I'll fetch some water and some bandages."

"Can you manage alone?" asked Mr. Armin. "If I'm quick, I may yet be able to catch the thief."

"Aye," I said, "go on. The others will be along shortly anyway." I ran down to the main room of the inn to fetch a ewer of water. As I was returning, Mr. Armin emerged from his room with a sword strapped to his side.

I was almost glad to have the duty of tending to Jack, for I did not care to think too much about the implications of what had happened. For one thing, if all the contents of the trunk were gone, that meant my mother's crucifix was gone as well. Even more troubling was the realization that, if the gatherer's box was here, then Jamie Redshaw must necessarily have been here, too.

I pushed these thoughts aside and forced myself to concentrate on Jack's wounds. He had been struck on the side of the skull with some blunt object—just one blow, as best I could determine. If it had been two inches lower, it would have hit his temple and most likely been the death of him. As it was, the effects were bad enough. The blow had torn loose a patch of his scalp, and the blood was welling steadily from the wound. If I was any judge of head injuries—which, in truth, I was not—the skull was surely fractured as well.

The first order of business was to staunch the bleeding. Gingerly, but rapidly, I clipped away the matted hair with a scissors from our medicine chest, plastered the flap of skin back in place, laid a pad of cloth on it, and bound the wound up tightly.

Before I had quite finished, Will Sly and Sam came trampling up the stairs, laughing over some incident from the afternoon's performance. They broke off abruptly when they saw the state of the room. "The devil take me!" said Will. "We've been robbed!" His eyes fell on Jack's unconscious form. "Is he dead?"

I shook my head. "Not yet, but near to 't, I'm afeared. 'A's leaked enough blood to fill a piggin."

"Have you any notion who did it?" asked Sam.

I did not wish to be the one to mention my father's name in connection with the crime. Nor, it seemed, did the others. Without a word, Will bent and examined the bare trunk and the gatherer's box. Then he stood and glanced at the doors to the room, both of which stood open. "The doors were this way when you arrived?"

"Nay. I unbarred the inside door to go downstairs. But the door to the gallery was wide open."

Will picked up the wooden bar, which was intact. "This door hasn't been forced. That means Jack must have unbarred it from in here. And that means—" He hesitated.

"It means," said Mr. Armin, who at that moment appeared in the doorway, "that whoever came to the door must have been someone well known to Jack."

I swallowed hard and said, "You—you saw no sign of the thief?"

"No," he replied quietly. His eyes met mine, and I saw something like pain in them, or pity. "But," he went on, his voice softer still, "I did find this, just outside the entrance to the inn yard." His right hand, which had been concealed by the doorframe, came forward, and in it was a wooden walking stick. The lion's head on the handle was barely visible, caked as it was with half-dried blood and tufts of human hair.

I shrank back from the sight, not wanting to look at it,

yet unable to take my eyes away. "Nay!" I cried. "It can't ha' been him, I'm certain of it!"

"I wish I could believe that," said Mr. Armin. "But look at the evidence."

"You look at it! You want it to be him! You've always disliked and distrusted him, from the day 'a joined the company!" I whirled and ran down the inside stairs, through the main room of the inn, and out into the street.

I stood there a moment, looking around frantically, for what I was uncertain—for some way out of this situation, perhaps. I wanted to run away, but there was nowhere for me to go. I wanted to find Jamie Redshaw, to ask him for an explanation, to warn him, but I had no notion where he might be. If he truly had played some role in the robbery—though I did not wish to consider that possibility, I must—then he would surely have fled or gone into hiding.

I began walking away from the inn with no destination in mind, only the desire to distance myself from Mr. Armin and from Jack's still form, from the empty money boxes and the bloody walking stick. I spotted the other sharers coming toward me, on their way back from the theatre. Abruptly I turned onto a side street. I could not bear to be the one to tell them all that had happened. Better to let Mr. Armin do it, I thought bitterly; he would get more satisfaction out of it.

As I turned another corner, I all but collided with Ned Shakespeare, who was emerging from an apothecary shop with a pouch of smoking tobacco. "You're in a hurry," he said. "Who's after you?"

"Ha' you seen me father?" I demanded.

"Not since before the performance. I wouldn't be surprised, though, if you found him at the sign of the Three Tuns." He gestured down the street. As I strode off in that direction, he called, "What's he done, robbed the box again?" I ignored him and broke into a run.

Ned was right. Jamie Redshaw sat at a table in the Three Tuns, intent on a game of primero. As I slid onto the bench beside him, he gave me a glance that did little to make me feel he was happy to see me. "Checking up on me, are you?"

"Nay," I said breathlessly. "I need to talk wi' you."

"Later, then." He laid two cards face down and was dealt two more.

I felt tears spring to my eyes and fought them back. "It's always later, isn't it?" I cried, my voice sounding choked and shaky. "This can't wait!"

He gave me a longer look now, his eyebrows raised. Then he turned back to his companions and laid his hand of cards on the table. "Prime, gentlemen. I'll collect my money in a moment." He took me aside. "What is it?"

Now that I had his attention, I was uncertain what to say. "The—the money," I managed. "It's gone. They think—they think you took it."

I had hoped for a reaction from him that would demonstrate his innocence—surprise, confusion, perhaps indignation at being falsely accused again. Instead, he scowled and muttered, "Damn! Are they on their way here?"

I shook my head slowly, but it was less a response to his

question than it was an attempt to clear the muddled thoughts in my mind, or perhaps to deny them. "I—I don't ken," I stammered. "I believe they think you've fled."

"And so I should, I suppose." He returned to the table and began to gather up his winnings.

I stood where I was a moment, dazed and dumb, and then tagged after him like a desperate beggar hoping against hope to be given some small bit of charity yet. "I can't believe—" I started to say. Then I broke off as the front door of the tavern was flung open and two men strode into the room. From his leather jerkin, I took one of them for a constable. The other was Mr. Armin.

Avoiding my gaze, he pointed an accusing finger directly at Jamie Redshaw. "That's the man."

The constable drew his sword and stepped forward. "You may as well come along peaceful, sir," he said, "and make it easy on yourself."

Jamie Redshaw hesitated, jiggling his coin-filled purse in his hand as if debating whether to turn and run or stay and fight. I watched him anxiously, uncertain which course I would have him choose. He chose neither. Instead, he shrugged and said, "This is poor timing, you know. I was winning for a change." Then he moved forward to meet the constable, who lowered the point of his rapier and smiled a little, obviously relieved that his prisoner did not mean to resist.

I felt a rush of relief as well, but with it came a sharp pang of disappointment that he would give himself up so meekly. Even if he was guilty, he might salvage some honor by putting up a fight or at least attempting to escape. But, I reminded myself, without his stick he had nothing with which to fight.

That situation changed abruptly. As the constable ushered his prisoner toward the door, Jamie Redshaw crowded him a bit. The officer knocked his knee against one of the benches. Before he could regain his balance, Jamie Redshaw swung his heavy purse upward in a swift arc. It caught the constable on the chin and sent him reeling backward. In an instant, Jamie Redshaw had seized the man's sword by its guard and brought the handle down across one knee, breaking its owner's grip.

Mr. Armin unsheathed his sword and came to the constable's aid, but a moment too late. Jamie Redshaw had turned to face him with the stolen rapier held at broad ward. "I've disarmed you before, and I'll do it again," warned Jamie Redshaw. "Let me pass."

Mr. Armin's reply consisted of a single word: "No." Then he closed in and their two rapiers clashed. Jamie Redshaw had no more to say, either; clearly, all of his concentration was taken up with turning aside Mr. Armin's blade as it darted in all directions, threatening first an edgeblow to the legs, then a *stoccata* to the stomach, a downright blow to the pate, an *imbrocata* to the chest.

"Stop!" I shouted, but of course they paid me no heed. I snatched up a heavy earthenware ale mug, meaning to launch it at someone's head, but I could not decide whose. If my aim was true and I managed to brain one of them, he would be at the mercy of the other. Though I did not wish to give Mr. Armin a chance to run Jamie Redshaw through, no more did I wish to let my father deal a deadly blow to my friend. In the end I could only stand gripping the handle of the mug, jerking it about this way and that in sympathetic movements, as though I were parrying phantom thrusts.

Under Mr. Armin's attack Jamie Redshaw gave ground again and again, unable to gain the offensive. Several times he tried the maneuver that had proven so successful in their previous bout, aiming the point of his rapier directly at Mr. Armin's sword hand. But now he did not have the element of surprise on his side. Each time Mr. Armin easily beat the blade aside and put him on the defensive again. -

The constable had gotten to his feet, rubbing his jaw, but he made no move to interfere. I am sure it was as obvious to him as it was to me that Mr. Armin was the more skillful scrimer and would win out in the end. The grim look on Jamie Redshaw's face told me that he realized it, too. The stiff way in which he moved said something more to me—that the wound in his hip was causing him a good deal of pain. Yet he fought on so doggedly despite it all that it hurt my heart to see it.

When Mr. Armin at last left an opening—deliberately, I am sure—Jamie Redshaw lunged forward. Mr. Armin did a deft traverse to one side and delivered a *stramazone*, or slicing blow, to his opponent's unprotected forearm. The stolen rapier clattered to the floor and Jamie Redshaw took several staggering steps backward, clutching the wound.

Without stopping to consider the consequences, I sprang

forward, swept up the fallen weapon, and came on guard before Mr. Armin. "Widge!" he said as sharply as a sword thrust. "Stay out of this!"

"I will not!" I cried. "Whatever 'a may ha' done, 'a's still me father!" Over my shoulder I called to Jamie Redshaw, "Go! I'll buy you some time, at least!"

"Just see that you don't buy it with your life," he replied, and then I heard his retreating footsteps. The constable seemed about to pursue him, until I blocked his path with my sword point.

"Step aside!" Mr. Armin ordered. "I've no wish to fight you."

"Nor I you," I said, my voice as unsteady as my sword hand.

He swung his sword suddenly, meaning, I am sure, to catch me off guard and disarm me. But he had trained me too well for that. I turned the blow aside and automatically countered with one of the *passatas* I had practiced so interminably. The point of my sword nicked his doublet, and perhaps his ribs as well, for he drew in a sharp breath.

I had never meant for us to come to blows, only to give Jamie Redshaw time to escape. I am certain Mr. Armin did not wish it, either. But sometimes, I believe, our instincts override our intentions, and so it was now. There may have been other, less obvious elements at work as well. Mr. Armin surely resented being challenged by one of his pupils, and for my part I was still angry with him for being so suspicious of my father; the fact that his suspicions were well founded only made matters worse. I may even have felt compelled to prove that I could acquit myself well in a fight that did not involve stage swords and moves planned in advance.

Whatever our reasons, we found ourselves striking at one another in deadly earnest. Though my breath came in panicky gasps and my blood pounded in my ears, I do not recall feeling frightened, particularly. My brain seemed numb, in fact. But my body responded as it had been trained to. I held my ground and gave as good as I took.

Mr. Armin had taught me that a skillful scrimer always looks his opponent in the eyes, for in that way he can read what his opponent will do before he does it. At first, the look in his eyes was hard and determined, but that quickly gave way to puzzlement, as if he were wondering how we could have let this happen. Then, suddenly, he scowled, and made a move I could not have anticipated: he stepped back and disengaged. "Enough," he said. "This is foolishness. I am not your enemy." He spread his arms wide, offering himself as a target for my sword. "Here. Run me through, if you will."

When I made no move to do so, he turned and stalked from the room. The constable took his sword from my unresisting hand and followed, leaving me standing there alone, feeling bewildered and bereft. No longer was I torn between two forces pulling me in opposite directions. I had succeeded somehow in cutting myself loose from them both.

I had not the slightest notion what I should do next. I could hardly return to the company, after having taken Jamie Redshaw's side against them. But I could not very well join Jamie Redshaw, either. Even if I could have swallowed my scruples enough to take up with a thief—and, if Jack should die, a murderer as well—I still had no way of knowing where he could be found.

Though I was not thinking all that clearly, I realized I was probably not wise to stay where I was. Once the constable learned that I was Jamie Redshaw's son, he might decide to clap me in irons as an accessory to the crime, or possibly detain me as a sort of hostage, a means of keeping my father from fleeing the vicinity.

I wondered whether Jamie Redshaw would, indeed, leave town without knowing what had become of me. Surely not, after I had risked my life on his behalf. Besides, he was wounded, how seriously I did not know. He might require a surgeon to tend to the cut on his arm; heaven knew he had plenty of money now to pay for such services.

The money itself might hold him here as well, at least for a time. There was a good deal of it, and all in small coins—too much for him to carry about comfortably, at least on foot. More likely he would look around for a horse to buy before he went anywhere.

These thoughts reassured me a little and set me in motion. I had somewhere to begin looking for him, anyway. When and if I found him, perhaps I could somehow convince him to make amends. Though he might be impulsive, I was certain he was not a bad man at heart. If I told him how urgently the money was needed to aid Sander and the boys, I might persuade him to give it up, or at least some of it. If nothing else, I would surely be able to retrieve my mother's crucifix.

But I was getting ahead of myself. My first task was to locate Jamie Redshaw, and my most immediate concern was that, if I had guessed where he was likely to be, then Mr. Armin would surely have done the same.

Keeping to the back streets and snickleways to avoid Chamberlain's Men and constables, I sought out the few local physicians and surgeons. None had treated a man with a sword cut recently. Late in the day, I inquired at the town's sole stables and was told that no one matching my description of Jamie Redshaw had purchased or hired a mount. In hopes that he might yet do so, I asked leave to lodge in the hayloft. The stable owner, a short, bandy-legged fellow, agreed to this; he even provided me with supper, in the form of one of his wife's meat pies. I would have offered to pay for it but that I had only a bit more than a shilling left from my wages, and no notion of how long it might have to last me.

The feeling of being all alone in the world was threatening to overwhelm me; to keep it at bay I engaged the man in conversation, asking if the plague had been a problem hereabouts. He said that, God be thanked, only a few townfolk had contracted the contagion, and those had been immediately confined in a pesthouse, thus preventing the spread of the disease.

We went on to talk of other things, including the performance of *Two Gentlemen* the stable owner had taken in that afternoon. Though I thought it best not to reveal my connection with the company, I asked him how they had acquitted themselves, in his opinion. "Quite well, overall," he said. "Not so good as the Admiral's Men, who were here a month ago, mind you. Not near enough laughs for my taste."

I nodded, and held my tongue, with some effort. According to Mr. Shakespeare, all the world's a stage; it seemed to me, rather, that all the world was a critic. "I can't fault the acting, though," the stable owner went on, "particularly the fellow who played the main bloke—Protocol, was it?"

"Proteus," I said.

"That's the one. I liked his lady friend as well—I disremember her name."

"Julia," I said—Sal Pavy's part, of course.

213

"You saw the play, too, then?" he said.

"Aye. Tell me, what did you think of Silvia—th' other lady friend?"

"Oh, she was good as well. Very natural."

Though it was hardly high praise, I was gratified all the same. I had not been overwhelmed with favorable comments on my acting lately. In truth, since we had set out on tour several months earlier, I had begun to feel that my command of charactery and my rudimentary skills in the healing arts were of more consequence to the company than my ability as a player. Yet with me gone and Jack out of commission for a good while—if, indeed, he lived—they would surely have trouble filling all the roles.

I wondered whether they would miss me. I was certain Sam would, and equally certain that Sal Pavy would not. The others would, I imagined, be regretful, but I had no doubt that, being practical men, they would not hesitate to fill my place with the first suitable candidate.

I forced myself to think no more on the matter. I could not bear it.

Jamie Redshaw did not turn up that evening, or the next morning, either. It would be a waste of time, I was sure, to look for him in the alehouses. But time was one thing I had a surfeit of, so I squandered it. Not surprisingly, no one had seen him since the previous afternoon.

I slept in the stable again that night. When I woke in the morning, it was with the certainty that Jamie Redshaw had departed, and so must I. If I could not salve my conscience by helping remedy the ills he had caused, I might at least return to London and do what I could to aid Sander and Tetty, Mr. Pope and the boys.

The stable owner pointed out the proper route, which led straight south. "When you get to Cheltenham," he instructed me, "turn east. That'll take you to Oxford and thence to London." He also sent me off with a full stomach, and another meat pie for the road.

I got as far as Upton before night fell, slept once more in a stable loft, and set out southward again in the morning. The miles went by slowly, with no companions to talk to. At first, out of old habit, I went over my lines in my head for the roles I was least sure of. But after a time I gave up on it. What was the use, when I had so little hope of ever playing those parts again?

I tried to pull myself out of the bog of despair into which I was slowly sinking by telling myself that perhaps I was better off this way. Perhaps I should think about finding a new career. There was no denying that acting was a tough and a thankless profession. It required so much hard work for so little return. It afforded not a groat's worth of security or stability. One could easily see why the sharers disliked and discouraged gambling; the everyday existence of a player was gamble enough without adding to it.

It occurred to me, then, that all these same things were true of life in general. Yet folk were not ordinarily eager to abandon it in hopes of finding some better alternative. To my knowledge there was but one other option, and not a very satisfactory one at that.

As tiresome as it is to travel in solitude, it is even worse on an empty stomach. I had had nothing to eat since the previous afternoon, save a little cracked corn I had filched from the horse trough at the stable in Upton. To make my misery complete, the skies, which had been as gray as my mood all day long, decided that since there was not a tree or any other shelter in sight, now was a good time to let loose with a deluge.

When I reached Gloucester at last, I was as wet and weary as I had ever been, with no prospect of anything better ahead of me than another night of sleeping on straw and a handful of horse feed to eat. So desperate was I that I might have turned my hand to begging, had there not been strict rules against it. Beggars were, like players, required to show the proper papers.

As I shuffled on my last legs down the street, looking for a place to lodge for free, I passed one of the thick upright posts that towns often provide for displaying public announcements. A familiar handbill tacked to it caught my eye.

A Performance of
the Pleasant Conceited Comedie
called
LOVES LABOURS LOST
by Wm. Shakesper

Plaide by the Right Honourable
the Lord Chamberlain his Servants
Lately of the Globe Playhouse, London

TO-MORROW 2 O'CLOCK

I am certain my mouth must have fallen open in surprise. The Lord Chamberlain's Men? Here? I had understood that, upon leaving Worcester, they would proceed directly east, to Mr. Shakespeare's home at Stratford. Perhaps the theft of the money had altered their plans. Perhaps they had decided, as I had, to return at once to London. Apparently they still were not overly concerned about Mr. Pope's plight, if they meant to waste a day in performing.

The stable owner in Worcester had said that I would come to a fork in the road here. I already knew which route to choose. I had not been prepared for this figurative fork in the road, though, and had no notion how to proceed. Should I seek out the company and ask their forgiveness? Or should I go on my way, making no attempt to reconcile with my friends—if indeed I could still count them my friends?

If I took the first course, would it mean I was somehow betraying my father? I was not sure it mattered; had he not betrayed me, after all, by using me as a means to insinuate his way into the company, and then making off with all our money?

After living most of my life without family or friends, I had only lately begun to learn about loyalty, so I did not yet know all it entailed. I wished to be faithful to my father, but if he had committed a crime I was not sure I still owed him any loyalty. Besides, what about my obligation to the Chamberlain's Men? In the hierarchy of loyalties, which came first—family or friends?

Though I knew little about the demands of honor or of

duty, I was well acquainted with the demands of the body and, unprincipled as it may seem, these were what finally swayed me. If the company took me back, I would at least have decent food to fill my stomach and a soft place to lay my head. Besides, if I did not rejoin them soon, Sal Pavy would surely usurp all my old roles.

All that remained was to find the players. If they had managed to put on a performance in Worcester, as scheduled, they might have made enough to pay for lodgings, so I checked at the first inn I came to. My friends were not there, but the host directed me to another inn, the Wheatsheaf. By the time I found the place, I was faint with hunger and fatigue and, despite the warmth of the evening, shivering in my wet clothing.

As I stepped from the dark outdoors into the main room of the inn, the light of the candles fairly blinded me. The smell of roasting meat filled my nostrils. Supporting myself against the doorframe, I surveyed the room, hoping to see a familiar and welcome face. To my painful disappointment, I recognized no one there.

Or nearly no one.

As I turned to leave, I caught sight of a figure that made me stop and stare: a fat-bellied man with an eye patch. Though he had his back to me, I was certain it was the same familiar-looking fellow I had seen weeks before, with Lord Pembroke's Men, and again at the tavern in Leeds, playing cards with Jamie Redshaw.

He was engaged in a game of cards now, with three other men. Piles of coins on the table told me that there was gambling involved. Apparently the one-eyed man was not faring well, for there was not a single coin in front of him. As I watched, he pulled something from his wallet and dangled it before the others, evidently offering it as a wager, in lieu of money. In the light of the small chandelier that hung over the table, the object in his hand glinted gold, and I gave a gasp of surprise, for even at that distance, I knew at once what it was—my mother's crucifix.

For a moment I stood transfixed while my brain, muddled by exhaustion, tried to work out what this meant. The cross had been in the company's treasury trunk; when Jamie Redshaw had stolen the contents of the trunk, he must have taken it, too. That meant he was here somewhere, or had been recently, long enough to lose the cross to the one-eyed fellow.

This realization set me in motion. I strode unsteadily across the room to the quartet of cardplayers and leaned over to get a closer look at the crucifix. There was no mistaking the ornate design. "Where did you come by that?" I demanded.

The man turned to me and, though his face was shadowed by his hat brim, I saw his one good eye widen in an expression I could not quite read. "What business is it of yours?" he said, between teeth that were clenched around a pipe stem. His voice was not the sort I expected from an actor. It had a rough, hoarse quality, as though he'd strained his vocal cords by shouting or was suffering from the grippe.

I knew I had heard that voice before, but it wasn't until he removed the pipe from his mouth and turned his head further, so the candles illuminated his face and neck, that I realized with a shock who it was that sat before me.

The eye patch and the amount of weight he had put on had fooled me. But the long, livid scar on his throat gave him away, for I myself had bound up the wound that caused it. "Nick?" My voice, too, came out sounding husky and uncertain.

He pushed back his chair and stood. "So, you haven't forgotten me, eh, Horse?" The grin on his face was not the sort that said he was happy to see me.

Hearing the old name with which Nick used to taunt me banished any doubt that it was, indeed, him.

"I—I heard you were dead."

"Well, that just goes to show, you can't believe everything you hear."

He pulled the eye patch aside. The eye beneath it was cloudy white, and the skin around it embedded with small, scablike flecks of black that I took to be grains of powder from the pistol that had backfired in his face. "Needless to say, I'm no longer playing girls, with this face . . . and this figure." He patted his expansive belly.

"But you're acting, still? Wi' Pembroke's Men?"

He laughed unpleasantly, and the other men at the table

joined in. "Sometimes we call ourselves that. This week, however, we're the Lord Chamberlain's Men, right, fellows?"

"That's right," said one of his companions, a bald fellow with a red, bulbous nose. He raised his mug of ale. "Don't you recognize us? I'm Will Shakespeare, and this here's Burbage."

"And this"—Nick stepped nearer me and clapped a rough hand on the back of my neck—"this is Horse. He's with a company who also call themselves the Chamberlain's Men. Isn't that a coincidence?" He seized a clump of hair on the nape of my neck and pulled my head back. "Where are your friends now, Horse?"

"I—I don't ken," I said.

"What do you *ken*, exactly?"

I jerked my hair painfully from his grasp. "I ken that crucifix belongs to me. How did you come by 't?"

Nick glanced at his companions, then shrugged. "Dishonestly," he said. "Would you like it back?"

I swallowed hard and nodded. "Aye."

"Well, then." His hand went to his waist and came up with a dagger. "You'll have to take it from me." He thrust the dagger at me, and I stumbled backward. "What's wrong, Horse? You don't want it after all?" He dangled the crucifix before me, daring me to reach for it. I glanced toward the door, gauging my chances of escape. "You want to leave, instead, is that it?"

"Aye."

"You want to return to the Chamberlain's Men, no doubt, and spill your guts about what you've learned. Well, I have a better idea." He advanced on me, the blade of his dagger moving in a slow circle that held my terrified gaze. "I believe I'll just go ahead and spill them right now. And this time, Horse, it won't be sheep's blood."

I kept retreating from the threat of the dagger and the menacing grin, until the backs of my knees came up against a bench. I lost my balance and sat down hard on my hucklebones. Before I could scramble to my feet again, Nick was leaning over me, with the blade at my throatbole. "No, no," he said, "I've just had an even better idea. Remember *Titus Andronicus?*" He jabbed the point of the dagger against my chin. "Stick out your tongue."

"Nay!" I choked.

"Neigh all you want, Horse. It won't save you. Come now, let's have your tongue."

Though my vision was blurred with pain and panic, I could see an indistinct shape move up behind Nick. Then the dagger jerked to one side; I felt it slice my skin and, though there was no pain at first, I cried out in alarm.

Nick was pulled backward, struggling and cursing. I slumped forward, holding my bleeding chin. I had to wipe away the tears that filled my eyes before I could discover who had dragged Nick off me.

It was Jamie Redshaw. He had seized Nick's right arm by the wrist and twisted it up behind his back so far that the point of the dagger threatened to puncture the back of

Nick's skull. With a bellow of pain and rage, Nick let the weapon drop. I had presence of mind enough to snatch it up and put it in Jamie Redshaw's hand.

He pressed the edge of the blade to Nick's throat and turned his hostage around so they faced the rest of the Mock Chamberlain's Men. "Stay where you are, gentlemen," he said calmly. "If we all keep our heads, then your comrade will get to keep his."

The bald, red-nosed man laughed. "In truth, we'd just as soon you did the blighter in." Casually he got to his feet and drew his rapier. "All the more money for the rest of us, you see." At his cue, the other men of the thieves' company closed in, too, with their weapons before them.

"Run, Widge!" Jamie Redshaw called over his shoulder.

"Nay!" I replied. "Not wi'out you!"

"I'll be right behind you! Now go!"

I turned to flee and then, remembering the crucifix, turned back and yanked it from Nick's grasp, snapping the delicate chain. As I headed for the door, I saw Jamie Redshaw plant a foot in Nick's back and send him reeling forward into his companions, who very considerately turned their swords aside to avoid impaling him.

With Jamie Redshaw at my heels, I dashed across the highway, nearly breaking an ankle in the deep ruts, and into the safety of the dark woods. "Hold!" called Jamie Redshaw softly. I slowed, and he caught up with me. "They'll not pursue us, I'm certain, for they're a lazy lot of louts. Let's sit down a while." Groaning slightly, he sank to the ground next to a broad beech, and I sat beside him, on a cushion of dead leaves that had escaped the rain under shelter of the tree.

"Are you hurt?" I asked.

"No, it's just the old wound acting up. What about you?"

"It's not a bad cut; I've stopped the bleeding. It would have been much worse, had you not come along. I should have done more to save meself, but I was too frightened."

"It's good to be frightened. It keeps you from being over confident."

"That's exactly the same thing Mr. Phillips told me about acting. You didn't seem frightened."

"I didn't have a knife at my throat. You acquitted yourself well enough—and even better back in Worcester."

It was the first word of praise I had ever heard from him and I held on to it as tightly as I held the crucifix. "How did you happen to be here, at the same inn wi' those miscreants?"

"I thought it might be worth my while to join their company—just temporarily, until some better opportunity should present itself."

"Join them? But . . . they're thieves!"

"Well," he said nonchalantly, "no one is without faults."

"How long ha' you been in league wi' them?"

"Just since your Mr. Armin chased me off. Oh, I had made their acquaintance before that and, as you may have guessed, sold them a few of your handbills."

"Oh." I had hoped he might reveal that the robbery was all their idea, that he had been only an unwilling accomplice. "What will you do about the money?" I said.

"The money?"

"What you took from the Chamberlain's Men."

"Oh. I'm afraid that's all gone."

"Gone?"

"I had a streak of ill fortune with the cards."

"You gambled it all away?" I said incredulously. "There must have been twenty pounds in that trunk!"

"The trunk? I never touched the trunk. I took no more than a few shillings from the gatherer's box."

"But . . . you brained Jack! We found your stick!"

"It's no longer my stick. Three or four days ago I wagered it on a hand of cards, and lost."

"To whom?" I asked, though I was sure I knew the answer.

"Richard."

"Richard?" I echoed in surprise. "Who is Richard?"

"Why, the very villain who so nearly cut your tongue out."

"Oh. That's not his true name. It's Nick. He was once wi' the Chamberlain's Men."

"And now he's taken to robbing them and burning their wagons? Nice fellow. I expect he deliberately left the stick behind to divert suspicion from him and his companions."

"No doubt. Tell me, in your time wi' them, did the name Simon Bass ever come up?"

"It did. I gathered that most of them were once players in a company run by Bass. How did you know that?"

"I'll tell you sometime," I said. "In the meanwhile, is there aught we can do to recover the money?"

"We might try asking very politely. Or, on the other hand, we might kill the lot of them."

Irked by his lack of concern, I said, "What about your honor? Do you not wish to clear your name?"

He laughed. "I'm afraid my only hope of having a clear name lies in taking a new one. Besides, you can tell your fellow players that I'm not the culprit. They'll believe you."

"I can't go back to the Chamberlain's Men," I said glumly. "Not after all that's happened."

"Of course you'll go back. What else can you do?"

I hesitated, like a player who is reluctant to say a line he has been given because he is uncertain how the audience will react to it. Finally I forced myself to say it. "I might go wi' you."

In the darkness I could not make out Jamie Redshaw's face, to read his reaction. I could only wait anxiously for his reply. It was a long time coming. At last he said, "No. You would not care for the sort of life I lead. I go where my whims or the whims of Fortune take me, and when I've overstayed my welcome, I leave. I get my living by whatever means I may. I cannot afford to concern myself with how honest it is. And I have as many ways of losing money as I have of making it. No," he said again. "It's no life for a lad like you, who can amount to something."

Though I listened to his words, I did not hear them. What I heard was that he did not want me. "But," I said, my voice trembling now, "even an I could return to the company, I could never go wi'out you. You're me father."

Jamie Redshaw blew out a long, heavy sigh, as though he had come face-to-face with something he had been making every effort to avoid. "As I said, honesty is not always my first concern."

If I had been stunned when he first claimed kinship with me, I was stricken now. "You—you lied to me, then?" I managed to say.

"Let us say, rather, that I misled you."

"But—" I held up the crucifix, which I still clutched in one hand. "You kenned me mother's name. You kenned it was carved on the back of this."

"A cozener's trick, nothing more."

"A trick? How—?"

"You recall the little man with half an ear? He and I were confederates, helping one another to relieve coneys of their excess coins."

"Coneys?"

"Gulls. Marks. Victims. He saw in you an opportunity for us to ally ourselves with a renowned—and profitable—company of players. I don't think he expected me to leave town with them."

"Nay!" I cried. "I don't believe you! You didn't lie to me then; you're lying to me now, so I'll go back to the Chamberlain's Men! You want to be rid of me!"

Jamie Redshaw did not reply at once. He got stiffly to his feet and brushed himself off. I could barely make out his dark form, silhouetted against the stars. "Well," he said, "as I've told you, I use whatever means I may." He turned away, then, and I heard his footsteps moving off through the damp, dead leaves, heading toward the highway.

I wanted to call out to him, to go after him, but I was afraid that, if I did, Nick and his friends might find us. In any case, I could not have found the words. There were so many questions tumbling through my mind, I could never have hoped to choose just one. Even if I had, and even if he had answered it, I would have had no way of knowing whether or not the answer was true.

Perhaps he had told me one true thing, at least. It was no doubt best to let him go back to his life, and I to mine. Whether or not we had the same blood in our veins, it was clear that we were cut from different cloth, he and I. If I stayed with him, I knew he would expect me to live by his rules, to behave and believe as he did, and I was not certain that I could, or would even wish to. But the heart does not always want what is best.

In the end I stayed where I was, curled up in the leaves at the base of the beech tree, partly because I was too exhausted to go on, partly because I feared that, if I came out of hiding, I might encounter the company of thieves, and partly, I think, because I still harbored some faint hope that Jamie Redshaw might return for me.

When it grew light enough to see, I found the road that would take me to Oxford and London. I was not certain how much help I could be to Sander and the boys. What they needed mostly was money, after all, and I had next to none. But I thought I might manage to find some sort of work. And in any case, I had nowhere else to go.

After I had walked along for an hour or so, a cart came by, loaded with casks of ale. "Going to Oxford?" asked the driver. I nodded. "There's room on behind if you care to ride—and if you care to help me deliver these kegs when we get there."

In Oxford I got a ride with another carrier, under the same conditions—that I help him unload his freight. By the time we reached London, three days after I left Cheltenham, I was so stiff and sore from being jostled about in wagons that I felt as though I'd been beaten soundly.

I took my leave of the driver at St. Paul's. I was shocked to see how quiet the courtyard of the cathedral was. Ordinarily the space was filled to overflowing with the booths of booksellers, stationers, and other vendors, and with folk come to buy their wares or just to mingle. Today there were perhaps half the usual number of sellers. The few folk who patronized them were not standing about casually, looking over the goods, as they normally did. Their movements were much more deliberate. They headed straight for a particular booth, made a hasty purchase, and departed again, avoiding as much as possible any contact with other customers.

Most of the business was at the booths of the apothecaries, and the liveliest trade was in plague remedies and preventatives—amulets filled with arsenic and mercury, tonics made of borage and sorrel juice, salves of egg yolk and swine grease. So far as I knew, no one at Mr. Pope's was in need of such nostrums. All the boys did, however, suffer from a chronic case of sweet tooth, so I stopped at a candy seller's stand and parted with a few of my own pennies in exchange for a bag of marchpane. I was so starved, it was all I could do to keep from eating the candies myself.

As I headed south toward the Thames, I noted that the traffic in the streets, too, was unusually sparse for such a pleasant summer's day. Many of those I passed were holding wadded kerchiefs up to their mouths and noses, like folk downwind of a dung heap; others wore twigs of rosemary in their hair. Though I put little trust in such measures, at the same time I felt uneasy, vulnerable, going about as I was with no means at all of countering the contagion.

Every so often I came upon a house that had been boarded up, and a cross nailed to the door, often with the words LORD HAVE MERCY UPON US scrawled beneath it. I hurried past these with a shudder, as though expecting some dread demon to spring from them.

At the embankment by Blackfriars, where ordinarily a dozen wherry boats were gathered, awaiting passengers, there were now but four. The wherryman who took me across instructed me to toss my penny into an iron pot that, he said, he would later place over a fire, to drive off the venom.

"The venom?" I said.

"That's how the plague is passed on, you know—through a poison, like snake venom, that seeps through a person's skin."

"Nay," I said, "I didn't ken that."

He leaned forward, but not too close. "Here's another tip for you," he said confidentially. "Don't bathe."

"Ever?" I said.

He shook his head emphatically. "It opens up the pores, you see, makes it easier for the venom to get in."

"Ah. Thanks for sharing that." I stifled a cough. It was obvious the man was following his own advice religiously.

After all the signs I had seen of the plague's presence, I was half afraid to arrive at Mr. Pope's lest I find a cross and a plea to God upon the door. I was relieved to see that the place looked the same as always—from the outside, at least.

When I stepped through the doorway, the boys, who were playing in the main hall, spotted me at once and descended on me like wild Irishmen, crowing with delight. As I fought to keep my balance under their onslaught, Goodwife Willingson came trotting from the kitchen, calling, "Whist, boys, whist! You'll disturb the master!"

I drew the bag of sweets from my wallet and dangled it over their heads. "This is for those who are quiet!"

When they had returned to their play, their mouths full of marchpane, Goody Willingson came to me and, seemingly about to break into tears, clasped both my hands in hers. "Thank the Lord you've come at last, Widge. I've been at my wit's end these past several days, what with Mr. Pope being ill, and scarcely a morsel of food to put on the table, and—oh, that's not the worst of it." She bit her lip and hung her head, as though she couldn't bear to go on.

"What?" I urged her. "What is it?"

"It's . . . it's Sander," she said. "He's gone."

I could scarcely believe I'd heard her right. "Gone?" I said. "How do you mean?"

"He went off a week or more ago, and he's not returned since."

"Did 'a not leave a message of any sort?"

"No, nothing."

"Did 'a take aught wi' him? Clothing? Food?"

"Not that I could tell."

I put a hand to my head, which had begun to throb. "Perhaps . . . perhaps 'a went out to try and find work."

"Well, he'd found something already, that's the thing. For a week at least he'd been going out several hours each day, but he was always home by dinnertime, bringing with him a few shillings or some food."

"Do you ken where 'a was working?"

She shook her head. "He never said. I suspect it was some lowly task he didn't care to admit to."

"That's not like Sander, though, to be so secretive."

"He's not been himself, lately. He's been distracted, like. To tell the truth, I believe he was hurt and disappointed that the company didn't respond to the letter he sent asking for help. I told him it might well have failed to reach you."

"It reached us, all right, but at the worst possible time. You see . . . every bit of money the company had was stolen."

She put a hand to her mouth in distress. "Oh, Law! They've sent nothing with you, then?"

"Nay. In truth, they did not even send *me*. I . . . I had a falling-out wi' them."

"Oh, Widge, no! What was the cause of it?"

"I'll tell you about it later." I dug from my purse the few coins that remained to me. "Here. That may buy a little food at least. Is Mr. Pope still under a physician's care?" Goody Willingson nodded. "How is 'a?"

"Up and down, like Fortune's wheel. For a time he seems

234

to be getting his strength back, and then Dr. Harvey comes and bleeds him, and he takes another turn for the worse."

I frowned. "How often is 'a bled?"

"Every few days."

"Gog's malt! It's a wonder the poor man has a drop of blood left to let! Has either of you asked this Dr. Harvey to leave off the bloodletting?"

Goody Willingson's look of surprise was as profound as if I'd asked whether they'd renounced their allegiance to the Queen. "Why, no! I'm sure the doctor knows what's best for him."

"Perhaps. I'll go up and see him."

"Yes, do. But mind you don't say a word about Sander. I've not told him yet. It might be best, too, if you don't mention the stolen money. We don't want him to fret."

When I looked in on Mr. Pope, I found him so weak he could scarcely talk. He had been such a vigorous man, despite his age, that it was shocking to see him so helpless. I sat by his bedside and, to spare him the effort of asking, told him all the things I was sure he would want to know about how the company was faring.

He reached out unsteadily to pat my hand. "I'm glad you're back," he whispered. He closed his eyes, then, and I thought he had gone to sleep. But as I rose to leave I heard him say, "Widge. Where is Sander?"

" 'A's just . . . gone out," I said, casually. "When 'a returns, I'll send him up."

As I stepped out into the hallway, I saw Tetty's slight

figure sitting on the top step of the stairs, looking down through the balustrade at the boys playing in the hall below. I sat down next to her. Without turning, she said somberly, "You came back."

"Aye," I said. "I had your picture to remind me."

"Good. You won't leave again, will you?"

I hesitated. I was not sure myself what I would or should do next. Finally I said, "Not for a while, anyway." I fished from my wallet some sweets I had saved for her. She accepted them as gravely as though they had been physicking pills.

Around a mouthful of marchpane, she asked, "Why did Sander leave?"

"I don't ken, exactly."

"Was it because we were bad? Some of the boys complained when there wasn't enough food."

"No, no," I assured her. " 'A would never stay away over such a trifling thing. There must be some more drastic reason."

In the morning I went looking for work, and found nothing. With the rising death toll had come a corresponding drop in business for the city's merchants and tradesmen. They were more inclined to let help go than to hire more. As I went about Southwark, I inquired of every familiar face I encountered whether they had seen Sander recently. No one had.

That afternoon, on a whim, I went by the Globe Theatre. All the entrances were locked. The only windows at ground level were those in the tiring-room. I grabbed the sill and hoisted myself up to peer inside. The place was, of course, as empty as a granary in May. Through the open tiring-room door, I could just catch a glimpse of one of the stage entrances and, beyond it, a small section of the stage itself.

The sight sent a stab of something through me—I was not certain what, but it was akin to the feeling I had experienced upon seeing again the orphanage in York where I had spent my early years. It was, I think, the curious sensation one gets when seeing a familiar place from a new perspective—from the outside, as it were, rather than the inside.

I had had no desire, of course, to be inside the walls of the orphanage again. But the sight of the stage filled me with a fierce longing. I dropped to the ground, wishing that I had not taken that look within. I knew that, in a month or so, when cool weather reduced the threat of the plague, the company would return and the theatre would reopen. What I did not know was whether or not I would be with them.

I sat on the steps outside the rear door of the theatre for a long time, hoping without much conviction that Sander might somehow be drawn back here. Finally, fearing that Goody Willingson and Tetty and the others would think that I had deserted them, too, I rose and, heavy-hearted, made my way back to Mr. Pope's.

28

The following day the physician returned to see to his patient. Dr. Harvey was a gaunt man with pasty skin. In truth, he looked as though he had been administering his bloodletting cure to himself, and had overdone it. Goody Willingson obviously knew the procedure well; she had already fetched a bowl. Dr. Harvey laid his patient's right arm across the rim of the bowl. Both Mr. Pope's forearms were dotted with small scars from previous bloodlettings. As the doctor opened his medical case, I got up the nerve to open my mouth. "Excuse me, sir," I said.

He gave me a cursory glance. "Who are you?"

"Widge, sir."

He selected a narrow-bladed scalpel from the case. "What's happened to the other boy, the tall one?"

"Sander." I glanced at Mr. Pope. "We . . . we don't ken, sir."

"What do you mean, you don't *ken*?"

"I mean, 'a's been gone a week; we don't *know* where."

"Hmm." The doctor took out a tourniquet and tied it about Mr. Pope's upper arm to make the veins stand out.

"I ha' a question," I said. "I understand that Mr. Pope's condition seems to grow worse after 'a's been bled."

"That's not a question," said Dr. Harvey.

"All right, then. *Should* his condition grow worse after 'a's been bled?"

"Yes, yes, that's to be expected. The patient always feels a bit weak at first from loss of blood. It's only temporary."

"But . . . well, is there not some other treatment you could try? One that would build him up, rather than making him weaker?"

Dr. Harvey sighed heavily. "The patient has suffered a stroke. That means there's a surfeit of blood, and *that* means it must be let out." He took hold of Mr. Pope's wrist and searched for a suitable vein to open.

I stepped closer to him. "But it would do him no dare, would it, an you left off bleeding for a week or so, to see what happens?"

The doctor turned to glare at me over the tops of his spectacles. "Do you have a university degree in medicine?" he demanded.

"Nay, of course not. I was only—"

"Well, I do. So stop trying to tell me how to do my job!"

Mr. Pope, who had lain quietly until now, somehow summoned the strength to sit up a little. His arm fell off the rim of the bowl. "Here," he said, his voice thick, as though he had drunk too much ale, "you've no call to be harsh with the boy. He's simply asking."

"Asking? What he is doing, sir, is questioning my ability."

"Nay," I said. "Only your methods."

"You must admit," said Mr. Pope, "the bleeding hasn't exactly been a great success. In fact, you might say it's been a bloody failure."

Dr. Harvey stood rigid a moment, looking as though he were contemplating letting blood from both our jugulars. Then he nodded brusquely and threw the scalpel carelessly back into its case. "Very well," he said, and untied the tourniquet so roughly that Mr. Pope winced. "Obviously, you don't want the care and advice of a physician. Go see an apothecary; he'll mix you up some fancy-sounding and foul-tasting concoction that is guaranteed to make you well. The catch is, you see, you can't ask for your money back if you're dead!"

"I wasn't—" I started to protest, but the doctor was already stalking from the room. I scrambled down the stairs after him. "I wasn't saying we should consult an apothecary. I only thought you might know of some other treatment."

"Well, I don't!" the doctor said sharply over his shoulder.

Angry and ashamed in equal parts, I trudged back up to Mr. Pope's room. "I'm sorry," I said. "I'll find another physician."

Mr. Pope waved a hand weakly, dismissively. "Sometimes common sense is the best doctor—and the cheapest, as well. Better we should spend what little money remains on food."

"But what an 'a's right? What an you've a surfeit of blood and something bursts?"

"Do I look to you as though I've a surfeit of blood?"

As I plumped up the pillows behind him, I studied his face, which was, as they say in Yorkshire, all peely-wally. "Nay. You look as though you're made up to play the ghost in *Hamlet*."

"Well, I'm not a ghost," he said. "Not just yet. Is there any meat in the house?"

"A little, I think."

"Then have Goody Willingson make me a cullis of beef broth, will you? Suddenly I'm starving."

The next afternoon, I went about the Bankside neighborhood again, asking after work and after Sander; I returned with little hope of finding either. To my dismay, I encountered Dr. Harvey coming from the opposite direction. I would have gone on by him without a word or a glance, but he stopped me. "I've something to tell you."

"An it's about yesterday," I said hastily, "I'm sorry I was—"

He held a hand up to silence me. "No, no," he said impatiently, "I'm not here looking for an apology. I wanted to let you know that I've found your friend."

"Me friend? Sander, you mean?"

Dr. Harvey nodded.

"Well . . . where is 'a?"

"In the pesthouse in Kent Street."

All the breath seemed to go out of me. With what little was left, I said, "The pesthouse? Where they take folk wi' the plague?"

"Yes. I look in there from time to time, and do what I may to ease their suffering. There's little anyone can do, except God."

Though the weakest parts of me, of which there were many, cried out against it, some small courageous part said, "I've got to go see him."

"If you do, you'll be in grave danger of infection yourself."

"So are you," I said. "Yet you go there regularly."

"I take precautions."

"Then so will I."

Dr. Harvey gave me a cloth bag filled with arsenic and instructed me to bind it to myself beneath my shirt and doublet, next to my heart. The theory behind this was that one venom repels another.

Folk fall prey to all manner of illness, of course, and as we made our way to the pesthouse I held on to the hope that Sander might not have the plague at all, but some other disease of similar symptoms. Perhaps, like Sam, he only suffered from the ague.

But when we entered the pesthouse and I saw him, that hope vanished. It took several moments for my eyes to find him, among the dozens of patients who lay about the room on straw mats. Even then, I was not certain it was he, so altered was his appearance.

The attendants at the pesthouse had burned his garments; he was covered only by a linen sheet pulled up to his chest. His arms were spread out at right angles to his body, like those of Jesus on the cross, so as to keep any pressure off the grotesque black pustules on their undersides. There would be similar painful swellings, I knew, on the insides of his thighs. His face was not pale and drawn like Mr. Pope's, but dark and contorted, as though he were slowly strangling.

"He's experiencing severe cramps," said Dr. Harvey dispassionately. "That's a mortal sign."

I gave him an angry glance, as though, by speaking of Sander's approaching death, he were helping to hasten it.

"I'll leave you alone with him," said the doctor. "It's best if you don't get too close."

What would have been best, I thought, was never to have gotten close to Sander to begin with. If I had not let myself come to regard him as my nearest friend, perhaps I would not feel now as though the arsenic in the bag I had bound to me were eating away at my chest and at the heart within it.

I knelt down next to his mat; the bay leaves and lavender and rose petals that were strewn about to purify the air gave off a scent that was spicy and sweet but not nearly strong enough to overcome the sour smell of sickness. "Sander?" I said.

He turned his head to the side with obvious effort; when his dull gaze fell upon me, he gave me a faint semblance of his old smile. "Widge," he said in a hoarse whisper. "You came."

I swallowed hard. "Aye." Though I had given up lying, I made an exception, knowing that it would ease his mind. "I've brought money wi' me—enough to provide for the household."

"Good. Good. I knew you'd manage it somehow. I hoped you wouldn't manage to find me, though."

"Why?"

"I didn't want you to see me like this. I wanted you to remember me as I was."

"I will, I swear." I fought back tears, wanting him to remember me, too, as I was in better times. I tried to think of something cheerful to say, but the question that was in my mind forced itself to the fore. "How did this happen? No one else in the household has come down wi' the contagion."

So faintly that I could scarcely hear, he said, "I had to get work, to keep the boys fed. It was all I could find."

"What was?"

"Carting the dead away for burial."

"Oh, Sander," I said.

He shrugged slightly, apologetically. "I followed your advice. I kept a kerchief soaked in wine over my face."

"Nay, nay, I never said it was certain proof against the plague!" I cried. "You should not ha' listened to me!"

With much effort he raised one hand, as though to clap me on the shoulder in his old familiar fashion, but then stopped himself. "It's not your fault, Widge. It was my choice. I'm certain that all of them"—he waved his hand

weakly to indicate the other patients in the pesthouse—
"tried the best they knew how to ward off the plague, and
it claimed them anyway. There's nothing anyone can do.
There are no rules to follow. It's all a game of chance."

I did not dispute him. I had heard other folk say the same
thing about the plague and about other sorts of ill fortune.
I think it gave them some comfort to believe it was so. It is
far easier to accept one's lot in life as inevitable, a whim of
fate, than it is to struggle and rail against it.

But I was not certain it was so. I suspected that, like
every other disease, the contagion had a cause, and if that
cause could be discovered the plague could be contained,
perhaps even cured. Surely, someday someone would un-
cover its secrets. But it would be too late for Sander.

I longed to do something to ease his suffering but, as
Dr. Harvey had said, there was nothing to be done. I had
seen Dr. Bright drain the pustules of plague victims and
apply ashes and quicklime to them, but the treatment had
seemed only to cause the patient more pain, and it made no
difference in the end.

I took my mother's crucifix from about my neck and
placed it in his outstretched palm. His hand closed tightly
about it, and he smiled faintly one last time. I fetched water to slake his constant thirst, but beyond that all I could
do was to sit by and watch him fade farther and farther
from me, as gradually and as surely as the evening sun was
fading from the sky.

I could not even arrange for a funeral, for at sunset all the day's dead were carted away at once and buried in hastily dug graves outside the city. I went along so that Sander would have someone to mourn him, and I marked the site with a small pile of stones, vowing to replace it someday soon with a proper headstone.

After the burial, I hurried home, knowing that Mr. Pope and Goody Willingson would be worried about me. To lessen the chance that I might carry the plague with me, I stripped off my clothing and burned it, and scrubbed myself all over with lye soap before I went inside. There was, unfortunately, no way I could avoid carrying to the others the sad news about Sander. I waited until the boys had gone to bed, wanting to spare them a while yet. I had hoped that, in telling Mr. Pope and Goody Willingson, some of the weight would be lifted from me, but it was not.

"I suppose I must let his parents know as well," I said. "Can you tell me where to find them?"

Mr. Pope shook his head. "In one of the shabby tenements along the south bank, I believe. Sander never told us much about them. It was my feeling that he was rather ashamed of them."

"I do recall him saying once," put in Goody Willingson, "that his mother made a bit of money taking in washing, and that his father turned around and spent it all again on drink." She clucked her tongue disapprovingly. "Imagine such a good boy as Sander coming from such sorry stock."

"Mr. Armin said to me not long since that it mattered naught what sort of heritage a wight had; the important thing, 'a said, was what you did wi' 't." I thought of Jamie Redshaw, and of my still unknown mother, and of myself. "Perhaps 'a was right," I said.

I had not yet spoken to them of Jamie Redshaw or of my reasons for leaving the Chamberlain's Men. I knew that, soon or late, I must, just as I must reveal to Mr. Pope that I had come to them almost empty-handed. But it would have to wait. We had all had enough dreary news for one day.

As I left Mr. Pope's room, I heard the sound of footsteps retreating along the darkened hall, and a door latch clicking shut. Someone had been listening in as I told of Sander's sad end. I had a strong suspicion who it was.

I opened the door to the room that Goody Willingson shared with Tetty. Though the young girl lay still in her bed, I could hear how harsh and rapid was her breathing. I sat on the edge of the bed and hesitantly laid a hand on her shoulder. "You overheard."

After a pause, she nodded. "I told you," she said.

"Told me? Told me what?"

"Every time I come to like someone, they die."

I shook her shoulder firmly, as though to dislodge this

notion. "Nay. Don't think that. You had naught to do wi'
Sander dying, I promise you."

She turned to face me, her dark eyes accusing. "You're a
good doctor. Could you not have done something to make
him well?"

"Nay. There was naught that could be done."

"I suppose you'll be leaving us now, too."

"I—I don't ken," I said.

"If you do stay, I won't like you. I'm never going to like
anyone again. It hurts too much."

I could not come up with a reassuring reply to this, for
the truth was at that moment I felt much the same way.
Yet I had to say something. I could not bear to sit helplessly
by as I had with Sander. I cleared my throat. "It doesn't
matter," I said softly. "I'll still like you."

Beneath my hand the tense muscles of her thin back
slowly relaxed. It seemed to me that for once I had managed to say the right thing. Perhaps it was not just what
Sander would have said, or Julia, or Mr. Armin, or any of
the others by whom I had measured myself in the past, but
it was what I felt and that, I supposed, made it the right
thing.

In the morning Goodwife Willingson sent me off to the
market in Long Southwark to see if I could prevail upon
one of the vendors there to let me have a bit of food on the
promise of future payment. She had exhausted her own
credit with them, she said. She hoped, however, that they
might be open to an appeal from a new face. But the mer-

chants were no fools; they knew me as a member of Mr. Pope's household, and knew that we were not likely to settle our account with them anytime soon. A fishwife did suggest that, if I returned late in the day, she might let me have those fish that had grown too fragrant to sell.

I shuffled home, feeling myself an utter failure. I had done nothing at all to aid Mr. Pope and the boys. All I had given them was yet another mouth to feed. I told myself that it would surely be better for everyone if I did not return to Mr. Pope's and, in fact, when I came to the house I walked on by it—to test myself, I suppose, to see if I could bring myself to leave.

I could not.

And a moment later I was extremely grateful for that fact. At the table in the kitchen sat a figure so unexpected and so welcome that I actually cried out, "Oh!" I had thought until that moment that crying out such things as "Oh!" was something that occurred only in plays.

Smiling, Mr. Armin rose and took my hand in both of his. "I hoped I would find you here," he said.

Finding me had not, of course, been Mr. Armin's sole purpose in coming. When the Chamberlain's Men reached Stratford, Mr. Shakespeare had raised fifteen pounds by collecting on some old debts, and Mr. Armin had been dispatched at once to London with the money.

"I'm to meet up with the company again at Bristol in four days' time," he said. "I hope you'll come with me."

"Truly? You've no sore feelings, then, over what happened?"

"Not any longer." He rubbed gingerly at his ribs. "I've a bruise the size of a sovereign where you stuck me, but my feelings are scarcely sore at all. It was natural that you should come to your father's defense."

I winced, for he had found a sore spot on me as well. "I'm not certain that 'a was me father."

"I always had doubts about it. One thing is certain, though—he was not the one who robbed us."

"I ken that. But how did you?"

"Ned Shakespeare told us how Jamie Redshaw lost the walking stick in a game of cards."

"Aye," I said, "and wait until you hear who 'a lost it *to.*"

Now that he was not being bled dry on a regular basis, Mr. Pope improved rapidly. Mr. Armin hired Goody Willingson's niece to help run the household until our return, and then we set off on Mr. Armin's new mount, to rejoin the company. By the time we reached Bristol I had recounted all that had happened to me since we parted ways, and Mr. Armin had managed to convince me that the company would welcome me with open arms and without reservations. Of the two undertakings, I believe the latter occupied the greater amount of time.

Mr. Armin had not deceived me, though. With the exception of Sal Pavy, who glared at me from afar, all the players seemed quite pleased to have me back. Even my old neme-

sis Jack greeted me with something resembling goodwill—
a tribute, apparently, to the effort I had put into patching
up his pate.

Sam seemed particularly glad to see me. Taking me
aside, he whispered, "Since you left, Princess Pavy has
been more unbearable than ever, and Toby is no help at all
against him."

"Toby?" I said.

Sam nodded toward the other end of the inn's main hall,
where a chubby-faced lad of thirteen or fourteen sat talking
with Mr. Phillips. I had assumed he was the innkeeper's
son or the stable boy or some such, but now that I looked
more closely I recognized him as one of the prentices from
the Earl of Hertford's Men, the company we had bested in
the acting competition.

"Oh, gis!" I muttered. "It's just as I feared! They've replaced me!"

Sam laughed. "You needn't fret. He's as wooden as a well
bucket, and twice as thick. They took him on only out of
necessity. We had no idea, after all, whether or when you
would return."

Sam's assessment of the new boy proved sound. Toby
was suited to play only the smallest and most undemand-
ing parts. However, Sal Pavy had laid claim during my absence to yet another of my customary roles, that of Blanche
in *King John*. Though I resented this liberty, I let it pass,
not wishing to seem ungrateful after the company had so
generously taken me back. But I could not help recalling
what Jamie Redshaw had said to me about Sal Pavy—that

he was the sort who would push and push until he pushed me out of the picture.

With his arm now free of the plaster cast, Mr. Shakespeare had no more need of my services; he could write the final scenes of *All's Well* on his own. Though I knew it was unfair of me, I resented this a little, too, feeling as though another of my old roles had been wrested from me.

My skills with a pen were still in some demand, for I had to translate into ordinary writing all the parts of the play I had set down in charactery, so the actors might decipher them. I had to rush the task a bit. The sharers wished to begin rehearsing the play immediately upon our return to the Globe, so that when we performed it before the Queen at Yuletide, it would be as polished as possible.

Now that the script was all but completed, Mr. Shakespeare seemed content enough with it, or at least resigned to it, as he was resigned to having an idle slouch for a brother. Though he trusted me, I think, to transcribe his work accurately, he was not above looking over my shoulder and goading me good-naturedly.

"I don't recall composing that line," he said. " 'He wears his honor in a box unseen that hugs his kicky-wicky here at home'? That's an abominable line. Are you sure you got it down properly?"

"Oh, Lord, sir!" I replied, pretending to be offended. "An 't sounds abominable, I take no responsibility for 't. I wrote down only what you told me to."

"But 'kicky-wicky'? What was I thinking of?"

"Nicky-nacky?" I suggested.

"Oh, certainly," he said. "That's so much better." Shaking his head, he turned to go, then turned back. "By the bye, Widge, when you copy out the sides, could you begin with Helena's? It's a demanding part, and I'd like to give him as much time as possible to study it."

"Him?" I echoed.

"Yes. Sal Pavy."

So stricken was I by his words that I lost control of my pen. It went skating across the paper, leaving a trail of ink like an open wound from which black blood welled. "Sal Pavy? You don't mean 'a's to play Helena?"

Mr. Shakespeare avoided my gaze. "We felt that he was best suited to the part."

"But . . . but I supposed that I would . . . " I trailed off.

Mr. Shakespeare spread his palms in a gesture of helplessness or apology or both. "I'm sorry, Widge. We have you down for Diana. It's a substantial role."

"But it's not Helena." The moment I said this I wished I had not, for I realized how petulant it sounded. I realized, too, that Mr. Shakespeare was likely to reply, "And you are not Sal Pavy."

He was not that unkind. He simply said again, "I'm sorry," and walked away.

It was difficult for me not to go after him. I wanted to remind him that, had it not been for me, the play would never have been put down on paper. I wanted to explain that I *knew* Helena, as surely as though I had watched her grow from infancy—which, in a way, I had. I had even been the source of some of the words she spoke.

But more than that, I felt a kind of kinship with her. Like me, she was an orphan; like me, she had been taught the rudiments of medicine; like me, she had offered her loyalty to a soldier and been rejected. She was plagued by the boastful and deceitful character now called Parolles, I by the boastful and deceitful character known as Sal Pavy.

There was one obvious difference between us, though. Helena had the courage and determination to pursue what she wanted until she got it. I, on the other hand, had stood by and let Sal Pavy steal from me, one by one, the roles that I had worked so hard to make mine, in the same way that Mr. Pope had let the doctor drain his life's blood from him a little at a time, without making a move to stop it, without even a word of protest.

Though I was as uncertain of my origins as I had been when we set out on the tour, I had not gone through all the trials of the past few months without learning something about who I was and what I was capable of. I had learned that, when the occasion demanded it, I could speak out against something I knew was wrong, that I could push aside my fears in order to aid a friend, that I could mend a broken arm or a broken head, that I could take up a sword in defense of someone I cared for. If I could do all that, then certainly I could stand up to Sal Pavy.

It was not Sal Pavy himself that I feared, of course; it was the possibility that if I upset the balance of the company, I might lose my place in it. But the fact was that, because I had failed to fight back, I was losing my place just as surely—not in one sudden fall from grace, but inch by inch, role by role. It had made the process more gradual, as being bled by a scalpel is more gradual than being skewered by a sword. If I was to be cut loose, I would just as soon it were done quickly.

Besides, unlike the subtle slice of a scalpel, a sword thrust may be parried. Jamie Redshaw had suggested that I counter Sal Pavy's attack by using similar tactics, by seeing to it that he met with a well-planned accident. But that was Jamie Redshaw's method, not mine. There were other, more civilized ways of fighting back.

That evening, while the rest of the company were gathering for dinner in the main room of the inn, I was searching through the costume trunk for a pair of long linen gloves that I had worn in the wedding scene of *Much Ado.* Then I waited, concealed upon the stairs that led to our bedrooms, listening for some line that would serve well as my cue. It came when Mr. Armin said, "Has anyone seen Widge lately?"

I made my entrance. I strode across the room and straight up to Sal Pavy, who sat as near to the sharers and as far from the prentices and hired men as he could get. Without a word, I flung down one of the linen gloves before him; it very nearly landed in bowl of stew.

Sal Pavy stared at me as though I'd taken leave of my senses—and he was not the only one in the room to do so. "What's this?" he demanded.

"Me gage," I replied.

"Your *gage?*"

"Me gauntlet, an you will."

He lifted the cuff of the glove distastefully, as though it were a worm, and gave an incredulous laugh. "You're challenging me to a duel?"

"Aye," I said. "An acting duel—to determine who will play Helena."

He gave another laugh, a rather uncertain one this time, and glanced around at the rest of the company. "Is this another jest? I'm afraid I don't see the humor in it."

Mr. Armin gazed curiously at me. "No, I'd say he's quite serious—resolute, in fact." He turned to the other sharers. "What do you make of this challenge, gentlemen?"

"Well," said Mr. Heminges, "if two c-companies may decide who will p-perform by m-means of a competition, I s-see no reason why two individuals should not."

"August?" said Mr. Armin.

Mr. Phillips shrugged. "It's bound to be more interesting than watching them shoot pistols at each other."

"Will?"

Mr. Shakespeare played thoughtfully with his earring. "We did tell Mr. Pavy that the part was his. If he does not feel he's up to the challenge, we can't very well force him to accept it."

All eyes were upon Sal Pavy now. His features remained so carefully composed that I could not guess what went on behind them. I was fairly certain he would not refuse me.

There was no way he could do so without looking foolish or white-livered. Besides, if I knew him he had every expectation of winning such a duel. He did not disappoint me. Putting on his most disdainful look, he tossed the glove back to me and said, "Name the time and place."

We settled on two days hence, at the Guild Hall in Salisbury, where we expected to be performing. Since we could not hope to con the entire part in that short a time, we limited ourselves to the final scene of Act I, between Helena and the Countess.

After Sal Pavy had retired to his stable, Mr. Armin came and sat down next to me. "So," he said soberly, "you've decided, as Hamlet says, to take arms against a sea of troubles and, by opposing, end them."

"Aye," I replied a bit defiantly. "I thought it was time I stopped retreating from Sal Pavy and took the offensive."

He nodded. "Well, I've only one thing to say in the matter."

"What's that?" I asked anxiously.

Mr. Armin leaned close to me and said sotto voce, "Why in all halidom did you wait so long?"

"Well, because . . . because I feared that, an I complained about Sal Pavy or quarreled wi' him, you and the others might—"

"Might what?"

"Might give me the chuck."

He patted my shoulder and said confidentially, "If we dismissed every member of the company who's ever been guilty of complaining or quarreling there would be no one left."

When I had been chosen the previous summer to play Ophelia before the royal court, I had had but one week to prepare for the part. It had been a trying week, filled with anxiety and self-doubt and sleepless nights. I believe I agonized every bit as much over this single scene from *All's Well*; the difference was, it was all of it crammed into two days.

Though I had never seen an actual duel, I doubted that the two combatants were expected to load their weapons and prepare themselves to kill or be killed while sitting within ten feet of one another. Sal Pavy and I, however, were forced to share the same small space behind the stage in the Guild Hall as we dressed ourselves and painted our faces and chanted our lines over and over like a paternoster under our breath.

I put my back to him and tried to ignore his presence, knowing that, if I gave him the opportunity, he would attempt to undermine my confidence or break my concentration. He did not wait for an opportunity. "You've put far too much cochineal on your cheeks," he said.

"Mind your own concerns," I muttered.

"Only trying to be helpful," he said innocently. "I didn't suppose you'd want to go out there looking like a fool." He glanced into the mirror and fluffed up his wig. "Or should I say *more* of a fool?"

I clenched my teeth. Let it pass, I told myself, and tried to think only of my lines.

"If you're determined to make a fool of yourself anyway, why not ask for the part of Lavatch? He's *supposed* to be a fool. And they're as likely to give it to you as they are to give you Helena."

I might have managed to let even this pass had I been striving still to be the good prentice, but I was not. I was striving to be Helena. I took the time to put the final touches on my makeup—and to count to ten—and then I turned to face him. "I suspect," I said evenly, "that your opinion of me acting ability is not nearly as low as you'd have me believe."

"Oh?" said Sal Pavy, clearly taken aback a bit. I am sure he expected me to respond with anger to his goading.

"An you truly felt I was no match for you, you would never have gone to so much trouble to try to get rid of me. It's only because you ken how capable I am that you consider me a threat."

"A threat?" He laughed, not entirely convincingly. "The only thing I've ever feared from you was that you would forget your lines and I would be forced to cover for you."

"You're lying. They say that no one may spot a lie like another liar. Well, I've been a liar most of me life. It's only lately that I've given it up."

"You may as well give up trying to compete with me as well, because you'll never win."

"We should not be competing at all, you and I. Theatre is

supposed to be a cooperative effort. Did they never teach you that at Blackfriars?"

For the first time his mask of superiority began to slip, giving me a glimpse of something darker and more vulnerable behind it. "No," he said. "But they taught me many other things, and one of them was that if I ever managed to get free of them I would not go back. I would do anything to avoid going back."

I nodded. I understood better than anyone the fierce determination he felt to keep his place within the company, at any cost. "I am certain that you want no advice of any sort from me, but I'll give 't to you all the same. An you truly wish to stay wi' the Chamberlain's Men, you'll never do 't through trickery and deceit; I ken that well, for I tried it meself. The only way you will ever belong is by being a hard and willing worker, and by being honest and loyal, so that you earn the trust and respect of the company."

"Trust and respect?" Sal Pavy sounded as though he were unfamiliar with the terms.

"You don't mean to tell me," I said, "that there was something you did not have at Blackfriars?"

Since he was the challenged party in the duel, Sal Pavy dictated the order in which we would perform. He chose to let me go first. As I stood by the curtain, waiting to go on, I felt unaccountably calm and confident. Mr. Heminges, who was playing the Countess to both our Helenas, came up next to me, adjusting his gown and wig. "Ready?"

I took a deep breath. "Aye."

He nodded encouragingly. "I b-believe you are."

Ordinarily when I made an entrance I was careful not to take much notice of the audience. It was easier for me to imagine, then, that I was living the scene, and not merely making a show of it. This time, though, I took a long look out into the hall. I was not playing to some mingle-mangle of strangers, come to lose themselves for a couple of hours in a world that was more interesting and exciting than their own. These were my fellow players, my friends.

An ordinary audience knew nothing about us actors, and cared less. Their only concern was for the fate of the characters in the play. But to these men—to Mr. Shakespeare and Mr. Armin and Mr. Phillips and Will Sly and even to Jack—I was not merely a player; I was a person. It was not enough, then, for me just to give them Helena. I had to give them something more. I had to give them me.

Always before, when I got well into a part, my awareness of everything outside the boundaries of the stage faded away. The only thing real to me was the world of the play. It was like slipping into a two-hour dream.

This time was different. I felt more the way one feels when he is just on the threshold of waking. Although he is still within the imaginary world conjured up by his sleeping mind, sounds and such from the real world intrude and influence the course of the dream.

So it was that, when I as Helena spoke of my father, images of Jamie Redshaw came into my mind. When I as Helena told the Countess, "You are my mother, madam; would you were—" I thought for a moment of my own mother, whom I never had known and never would. And when Mr. Heminges as the Countess remarked upon the tears that filled my eyes, he did not have to imagine them; they were there.

At the conclusion of our scene, we received an enthusiastic round of applause from the company. Under cover of it, Mr. Heminges said to me, "Well done, Widge." I could not help but agree.

Now that I had taken my shot, it was Sal Pavy's turn. I was not certain I wanted to watch. It would be like watching an opponent in a duel level his pistol at you, and wondering whether or not you would survive. In the end, I sat close behind the curtain and listened.

He made a strong beginning. His Helena was more forceful and vibrant than mine, who, though strong-willed, was soft-spoken. He was clearly determined to make my portrayal seem pale and anemic—and he seemed to be succeeding.

But a few minutes into the scene he lost momentum somehow. It was as though some part of his mind was occupied with something besides the role—perhaps with the conversation we had had not long before. Well, I had meant to give him something to think about, but not necessarily now. When he came to the line "My friends were poor but honest," he seemed to falter and forget where to go.

Out of old habit, I threw him the next line, but he failed to take it. Thinking he had not heard, I repeated it, more loudly. Still there was only silence from the stage. I peered through the opening in the curtain. To my surprise, Sal

Pavy was not facing his partner in the scene but had turned to look out at the members of the company who formed the audience. "The lines seem to have left my head," he told them. His voice was steady; his head was held high. "I could do a bit of thribbling, but you would know. I prefer instead to concede." He made a dignified bow, turned, and walked off the stage. A generous burst of applause followed him.

Suspecting that Sal Pavy would prefer to be alone, I ducked around the curtain and joined my friends, all of whom congratulated me warmly. Actually, Jack's comment could probably not be considered warm. What he said was, "I could never con that many lines in two days." It was, I supposed, the best I could expect from him.

Mr. Shakespeare said, "With you as Helena, perhaps this will not be such a poor play after all."

Mr. Armin gripped my hand almost painfully hard. "Don't think for a moment," he said, "that you won only because Sal Pavy conceded defeat. It was your performance and nothing else. It was astute, it was assured, it was affecting."

I did not know what to say. Fortunately Mr. Armin covered for me. "You know," he said, "when an actor truly shines in a role for the first time, we say that he's found himself. Well, it seems to me that you've found yourself. How does it feel?"

I thought of a line at last, one that would fit any situation. "Oh, Lord, sir," I said.